The Ants of Trescotham Hall

Anne Braid

DEDICATION

To Molly and Phoebe with love. A new generation of strong girls.

CONTENTS

ACKNOWLEDGMENTS

Love and thanks to Kim and Molly for all of your valuable input.

1 Seeing Stars

As she slowly opened her eyes, she could see beyond the beautiful clear blue sky to the incredible shimmer of the outer atmosphere and the faint glow of light from the myriad of stars beyond. She lay still for a moment taking in the stunning view.

She knew that some of the cacophony of sound that gently vibrated her eardrums came from the hidden world living in the grass around her head. She filtered most of it out, as she had always been able to do, until she heard someone in the distance calling her name and heard their familiar footsteps running towards her.

She gingerly tried to sit up and felt the pain down the left side of her face and mouth. She could taste metal and her lip was already starting to swell. She was just checking that all her teeth were still in place when her brother finally reached her.

'You were some help'

'Well I thought you were running behind me. It was your own fault, anyway. You can't keep your big mouth shut, can you? You couldn't just leave them to it and mind your own business for once.'

'No, I couldn't! We all use that play area and that broken glass could have hurt someone.'

'Yeah, well it ended up hurting you!'

'You know what I mean. Ouch! What does it look like?'

'You've got blood between your teeth and a fat lip and your cheek looks a bit red. Good job you're a quick healer. Which one of them hit you?'

'The girl did. The two boys grabbed my arms and she socked me one before I could get away. I don't know how they took me by surprise. I can usually read people better than that but I think I must have got distracted when that little girl screamed when she fell off the swing '

'Ha, so I need to distract you to stop you reading me then do I? It's always annoying when you seem to know what everyone's thinking. At least it was only your face she hit and that can't be made to look any worse!', he said, grinning.

'Thanks a bunch, now help me up. We'd better go tell Mum'

****

'Mum!! A stupid lass has just hit Molly in the gob'

'It's mouth, not gob!! Come here and let me have a look. Are you ok?'

They both explained what had happened.

'Next time, run home first and tell me what's going on, or tell a nearby grown up, instead of tackling them yourself. Pity they don't go to your school or I'd love to show them what it's like to be bullied by someone bigger!'

'Mum!!!!'

'I know!! I know!! I'm only thinking out loud. That would NOT be the right thing to do. There, I've cleaned your lip up a bit. Rinse with this salt water. It won't kill you.' She said as Molly pulled a face. 'Good job you're a quick healer'

'That's what Harry said, but it still hurts at the time'

'Ok. I don't think there's any permanent damage. Good job it was only your face'

'WHAT is WITH this family?'

Kim laughed.

'Dad will be getting up in half an hour. I don't think he's had much sleep today and he's going into work early tonight, so keep the noise down. Lucas is playing on the Wii so don't all start falling out and waking Dad up, please.'

'Ok Mum'

2 THE LETTER

It was the next day, when the children had gone to school, that The Letter arrived.

It looked very grand. It was on good quality thick paper of a creamy colour and had a crest in the centre at the top. It was from somewhere called Trescotham Hall. Kim had never heard of it and she doubted Mark had either.

'Dear Mr & Mrs Clayton

I would like to invite you to bring Molly along for an informal chat about her future, at your convenience. Please call the number above to arrange a suitable time and please bring this letter with you.

I would appreciate it if you would not discuss this letter, or the appointment with anyone else, including Molly, until our meeting.

Yours sincerely

Beth Drake

School Principal'

Kim felt a bit uncomfortable, but definitely curious. Why all the secrecy and what exactly was Trescotham Hall? 'School Principle' presumably meant it was a school of some sort. Obviously!.... but what sort? There was no way they could afford to send Molly to a private school so that was out of the question. She was only eleven so it was far too soon to think about further education, like college or university, even though it was clear she was extremely intelligent.

She couldn't exactly ask other mums if their children had received such an invitation. After all she had been asked not to discuss it with others. She made herself a coffee whilst her computer was booting up. She would Google them first to learn as much as she could before she decided whether to make an appointment or not.

Trescotham Hall, Trescotham, nothing came up that looked anything like the right website.

'Curiouser and curiouser, cried Alice' Kim said out loud, quoting from one of her favourite books. Why is their website so hard to find. Perhaps they haven't got one, which would be even more astonishing.

She picked up The Letter again. No address for them either. She hadn't noticed that. It was addressed to both of them so at least she could discuss it with Mark when he gets up. If she could wait until then.

She was tempted to call her own mum. She was the most likely to have heard of Trescotham Hall. She had always amazed Kim and her sisters with her vast knowledge, which she told them came from reading so much. She did spend ALL her time on her Kindle, with her nose in a paper book or on the internet.

Mum was such a tech head! She loved all types of technology and often said how frustrated she was that it was not even more advanced. She said she had been born too early and was really annoyed that she would miss all the fabulous new tech of the future. The girls thought she was a bit crazy sometimes but they always trusted her judgement.

Kim was starting to feel obligated to tell her. After all, she had always told her girls, 'If anyone ever tells you to keep a secret you're not comfortable with, ALWAYS tell me'. Kim knew this was to protect them when they were children, but she also knew her mum could be trusted with any confidence.

Kim finally decided to follow the request in The Letter for now and to call the number first. Perhaps she could find out more over the phone and perhaps get the correct website address. She checked the calendar first to find a date and time that both her and Mark would be free. IF she was happy with what they told her, of course.

Excellent, Mark had a week off in two weeks time and she had kept her diary free in case they wanted to do anything for the half term. Mum would look after the boys. She didn't know how long they would be until she knew how far away it was, so she dialled the number to find out.

3 THE PHONE CALL

'Hello Mrs Clayton. This is Beth Drake speaking. Thank you for your call.'

'How did you know it was me calling?'

'Oh, I'm so sorry. I know how unnerving that can be. Your name and number came up on my screen.'

'But I've never given you my number'

'Don't worry, Mrs Clayton, it's nothing sinister. We have highly sophisticated software which, amongst other things, matches names to phone numbers so we always know who is making calls to us'

'Mmmmm…. Maybe more paranoid than sinister?'

'Perhaps it appears so, but the security of our students is of paramount importance to us'

'You are a private school then. It's just that The Letter didn't really say much and I couldn't find your website and what with being asked not to discuss it with anyone, even Molly…………'

'Yes, I understand how mysterious this must seem to you, but I assure you such precautions are necessary. All will become clear at our meeting.'

'Can I please have your website address then so I know how to find you?'

'I'm afraid that won't be possible. If we can agree a date and time today, I will arrange for directions to be sent to your phone just before you depart'

'But how long should the journey take and how long will the meeting be? I need to tell my mother as she'll be looking after my other children.'

'Don't worry, Mrs Clayton. I'm sure Sarah won't mind having the boys for the whole day. Now let's sort out that appointment'

4 THE TEXT

Kim hadn't slept well. They must be crazy taking Molly to.....where? and why? And meeting who? When she did sleep, she'd had fitful dreams of the three of them being kidnapped and held in a dark, dank cellar and the boys all grown up and saying 'I wonder whatever happened to Mum, Dad & Molly all those years ago'.

At least she would have Mark along with her for support and by morning she had decided to write a note to her mother explaining events so far. She would put a copy of The Letter with it and hide it at home, just in case. This made her feel only slightly better.

The boys knew they were spending the day at Nan's and that their cousin Ethan would be there as well, who lived next door to her, so they were all getting rather noisy and over excited. Mark was snapping at them to calm down and Kim gave him an understanding smile as she knew he was feeling just as nervous about the day ahead as she was. Then beep, beep, a text arrived.

****

Molly was not at all surprised when her Dad told her to get back in the car when they got to Nan's and that the three of them were going somewhere together. She had sensed for weeks that something was building up to today but she couldn't quite get a handle on the specifics.

She knew it was wrong, but she had tried to listen in on her parent's conversations to try and find out more, but they had learnt long ago to wait until Molly was asleep before discussing anything important. She couldn't wait to get rid of the boys so she could find out where they were going.

Finally, they were ready to leave! Molly bombarded them with questions before the car doors were even closed. 'Just wait a minute and I'll tell you as much as WE know, while Dad drives'. Molly became more excited as her mum told the events so far since receiving The Letter.

'Wow, do you think they want me to go to their school? Would I have to live there? I wonder what it's like'

'Don't get your hopes up, Molls.' said Dad. 'However much it costs will be far more than we can afford. These private schools cost a fortune and I can't work any more hours than I do already and neither can

Mum, until you guys are much older. I don't know why they want to meet us but let's just try to enjoy a day out together. Make the most of getting your mam & dad to yourself for a change!'

Molly sat back and looked out of the car window. The wintry green fields flashing by barely registered in her consciousness as her mind went into overdrive. They should be there in another half an hour or so according to Mum. How come no one had heard of this school if it was so close to home? How come they had no website? Not one that could be easily found at least.

Mum was a bit freaked that they had found her phone number so easily as she was ex-directory, and the lady she spoke to had her mobile number too for the text. She hadn't put either of them on Facebook of course so as far as Mum knew, only family and friends had her numbers. She'd said she thought there must be some law against them getting hold of private numbers so easily.

Molly knew both of her parents were more anxious than they would admit but *she* felt more exhilarated than worried. This felt like a real adventure to her and after all, she had always loved a good mystery story.

5 GOING WHERE?

'If they'd have given us the post code or even the address, I could have put it in the Sat Nav. It would have been much easier, instead of 'turn here, turn there' and having no street names to confirm we are going down the right road.' Mark grimaced in frustration.

'You just drive, love, and I'll try to get us there. It must be somewhere round here. We've just come through a village called Laceby but we still may be totally in the wrong place. It says 'Go two and a quarter miles and turn right between two white boulders which mark the beginning of the driveway. The gate will open automatically for you. Drive a further six miles and I will meet you at the steps to the Hall.' Drive slowly along here, love, in case we miss the entrance'

'I can see it through the trees, Mum. It's a huge stately home like the one in that Jane Austin drama we watched the other night. '

Kim was about to comment that she couldn't possible see for 6 miles and remembered which of her children she was talking to.

They would have missed the entrance altogether but Molly spotted the white rocks as they turned the last bend. Mark was really pleased there were no cars behind him as he swerved abruptly right.

'You'd think a school would have a board at the entrance proudly telling you their name,' he said as they waited for the drive gates to slowly follow their well worn curve and let them through. 'And how did they know we would be here at this precise moment?'

6 SURPRISE AT TRESCOTHAM HALL

Beth Drake was waiting on the steps as they drove up to the stunning stately home. She was much younger than they had expected, maybe only in her early thirties. She was very petite and very beautiful with big brown eyes and long red hair which reached almost to her waist.

She was smartly dressed in business attire consisting of a black pinstripe skirt, that sat just at knee length, a green silk shirt and a short black double breasted jacket. She wore stunning green shoes which laced part way up her calf. She had put accessories together that gave her a certain style all of her own and made her look young and trendy, yet extremely classy.

She had sent a young woman down to take their keys so that she could park the car for them and after formal introductions she led them inside.

'I think we'll be more comfortable in the library. I've asked for some refreshments to be brought in to us in there'

They walked across such a huge hallway that would have held their entire house three times over! It was oak panelled and an amazing staircase, which looked like it was simply floating in mid air, was the centrepiece. Beth opened a huge oak door and invited them to step through into the library.

'Wow, my Mum would ADORE this room. She's always said, if she won the lottery she would have a house with a library and she then describes this exactly!' said Kim.

It was indeed a beautiful yet cosy room. It had, of course, wall to wall bookshelves, crammed with all sorts of tomes. There were several special ladders on runners for reaching the upper shelves.

The room was very light and airy, as at each end, there was an almost floor to ceiling bay window with beautiful views across the rolling countryside. At the base of each window were very comfy looking window seats with soft turquoise cushions.

In the centre of the wall facing them was a huge 'walk-in' fireplace with logs stacked high on each side and a huge grate in the centre, full of crackling burning flames which was very welcoming on such a bitterly cold day.

In front of the fire were three soft turquoise overstuffed sofas in a u shaped configuration with a range of co-ordinating cushions scattered on each. In the middle was a very old, but well polished coffee table on which a tray of hot drinks was just being placed.

When they were all sitting comfortably with their warming drinks and were starting to be mesmerized by the dancing flames in the fireplace, Beth got down to business.

'I'm so sorry about the cloak and dagger but I hope you'll understand why, when I tell you a bit more about us and why I've invited you here. I hope you'll listen with open minds as some of the things I have to tell you all, you may find a bit difficult'

Kim and Mark felt a bit uneasy but waited patiently for her to continue. Molly just felt excitement.

'First of all, let me start by giving you some background about how we started up, ten years ago now. Our founding members envisioned a totally different school from the one we have today. They were very concerned that young women were still not being given the opportunities that legislation had promised and we were still very far from a truly equal society.

They wanted to provide advanced education and training for specially selected girls with the aim to get them into highly placed, lucrative jobs, where they would have influence to change things.

They also wanted to admit selected boys too. Those who it was felt were in danger of being brought up with old stereotypical attitudes to females, so that they could work alongside each other.

They hoped to produce young people that were not only skilled in many different areas but also had a more respectful, understanding attitude to others in all walks of life.'

'That sounds like a great idea to me' said Kim - and like something my mother would get involved in, she said to herself, her face betraying those thoughts as they whirled around her mind.

Beth paused for a moment before she continued.

'This is probably the best time for me to reveal something to you. I've had permission from your mother Sarah, to tell you that she is, in fact, one of the founding members of this school.'

Kim was stunned, yet it explained so much. She wondered if, on some level she had suspected all along that her mother was involved. But why had she kept this from her for all these years?

7 MOLLY'S GRANDMOTHER

Sarah Thompson was the middle child of three daughters born to Zena and Albert Thompson. Just before her eighth birthday her whole world was shattered when her mother died of a brain haemorrhage on Boxing Day that year.

This was the mid 1960's when most men were the bread winners but rarely had any involvement in child care. Her mum had worked from home, mending fishing nets to help supplement her dad's meagre pay as a railway worker, but she had also been the girl's main care giver.

It was very difficult for Albert to act as both mother and father, with very little help available to him as a single parent in those days. He was of the generation that would refuse any help from the welfare anyway as they had too much pride to accept it. He even refused free school dinners and sent the girls to school every week with their full dinner money.

So he brought his girls up alone. He was given 'compassionate hours' by his employers British Rail, instead of having to work unsociable shifts. This enabled him to be there to get the girls off to school and get back just after they got home, but it also meant a considerable drop in income without the shift pay and overtime. Relatives helped out initially until the girls were old enough to be left on their own for an hour each day.

He eventually qualified as a train driver and passed all of his exams with flying colours, despite having left school at age 14. Money was still very tight though, so there were no luxuries but the girls never went without hot, healthy meals.

It wasn't until Sarah left school and went into the working world that she realised she had even more to thank her father for. She had never before realised that in the adult world, she would be thought of as less because she was a woman! That was the impression that she got. Her father had never treated her or her sisters like that. She didn't understand why there was a double standard that meant females were less and males were more! Surely they were all individual people with different thoughts and dreams, but to divide people into 'more' or 'less' depending on gender, didn't make any sense to her at all.

Of course there had been a couple of signs when she was at school. One was when she asked to join the rugby team and was told she couldn't because it was too rough for girls. She tried unsuccessfully to challenge this theory stating that her physique was not much different to some of the boys that were in the school team, and she was a much faster runner.

She also challenged why the girls were only allowed to run up to 800 meters in the track events, when the boys ran up to 1500. Although she didn't like running the longer distances herself it seemed total, inexplicable, nonsense. She just put it down to an idiotic PE teacher and it never entered her head that these were symptoms of the wider world.

By the time she met her much loved husband Garry she was working in a bank. As she was planning the wedding, she was told by her supervisor that she had to write a letter to her head office to ask if she could keep her job once she was married. She was furious! She was told to be grateful because the rules had only just changed and only a few months before, women who got married had to leave work altogether! Thankfully things were about to change again.

She was still battling against this concept of dual worth and dual standards, when the impending Sex Discrimination and Equal Pay Acts were all over the news. This was 1975 and she couldn't believe this was only just coming into force. She was sure this had happened in the 1920's. Her mind went back to one of the rare times her father had lost his temper with her.

She had been trying to delay bedtime when her sisters had already gone up, so she started asking him about the up-coming elections. Although she had tried this ploy many times before, she really did enjoy listening to her father's views on many subjects including politics. She particularly liked taking the opposite view just to be mischievous and rile him, even though she often secretly agreed with him.

On this particular occasion she had made the mistake of saying that all the parties were as bad as each other and she didn't intend to vote at all. She saw real anger on her father's face that night, which startled her.

He told her about Emmeline Pankhurst and the Suffrage movement and that women had died to give HER the right to vote and how DARE she throw that precious right away.

From the age of eighteen, she never once neglected to cast her vote and was very proud to do so, but looking back, she thought she must have naively assumed the right to vote meant the right to be treated as an equal.

It was over the next couple of decades, when total equality still seemed so elusive and the next generation of girls were taking advantage when it suited them (to get out of the heavy lifting, so to speak), instead of trying to change things, that the seeds of the school started to form.

8 THE SPEECH

Sarah had honed her people skills at the bank and had also been the union representative, which she loved. It was at one of the biennial union conferences that her temper got the better of her, once again and she felt she had to say something. She got up to give an impromptu speech that was to change her life and start her on the road to realising her dream.

She had always been good at standing in front of a crowd and saying what she thought without a script. It may have been her passion that made the words tumble out in the right order and she was rarely nervous. She had spoken on various issues before at previous conferences.

She didn't know it at the time, but this was to be her last ever conference. She wasn't down to speak on this particular issue but when she had heard some of the previous speakers she got more and more agitated.

The union had recently created a black workers' section and a women's section, they said 'to address the needs of these groups'. Sarah had already made her feelings known about this to the union secretary but it didn't seem to be a popular view.

The speakers were discussing the upcoming black workers' conference and one commented, 'wasn't it great that two black people, Denzel Washington and Halle Belle had won Oscars that year and the awards were being nicknamed 'The Black Oscars'.

Sarah jumped up and waited in line to speak. She listened to more speeches about how forward thinking we all were by creating these special sections of the union until finally it was her turn to step up onto the podium.

> *'Hi, as some of you will know, my name is Sarah Thompson.*

> *First of all, I would like to ask for a show of hands around the room and also on the top table behind me. How many of you think that we are all treated as equals by our employer and by our union?'*

Unanimously, green 'FOR' tickets were proudly held in the air and the top table all nodded assent.

> *'Excellent...... Except I disagree. Our union does not believe we are all equal and neither do most of you in this room and I'll prove it to*

you. How would you feel if the union organised a 'White Man's Conference'?'

She paused for a few seconds to let this sink in and heard the mutters of disapproval around the room.

'Well, I for one would be furious. I'd say, 'Why are the rest of us excluded? Who do you think you are? Do you think you're better than us?

So why aren't we saying the same about the proposed Black Workers' Conference and why aren't we equally cross about the new women only section? Is it because we all really think these groups ARE inferior so need specialist help? We're acting like we do.

We all have individual needs, even white men.'

(Titters around the room)

'There has been mention of the 'Black Oscars' today. These actors won their awards for being the best at what they do. ONLY when the colour of their skin does not even warrant a mention and ONLY when we have no need for a womens' section or a Black Workers' Conference, ONLY THEN will we have TRUE equality. Thank you.'

There was silence as she stepped off the podium. She was used to her opinion not always being appreciated but she still needed to be heard. She had once been accused of being a 'trouble maker' for pointing out something that was just plain wrong. Her answer to that had been, 'Sometimes trouble needs making'.

But, before she even managed to reach her seat, the whole conference hall erupted and she got the longest standing ovation that anyone could remember in the union's history. People were shaking her hand and patting her on the back and it took her a while to get back to her seat and for everyone to settle back down.

As they broke for lunch she was still being congratulated when the president of the union approached her and said that she was going to put forward a motion that these sections of the union be disbanded. Sarah was thrilled.

9 FORTUITOUS MEETING

She also had another very interesting discussion that lunchtime. Several invited guests had been seated at the back of the hall from all walks of life: business leaders: other unions: politicians. One of these guests, a very tall, elegant lady, approached her in the lunch queue and asked if Sarah would mind if they ate lunch together as she had something important to discuss with her.

'Yes of course, I don't seem to know as many people at this year's conference.'

'My name is Lady Catherine Sampson but please call me Kate. I've saved a quiet table in the corner, if you'd like to join me when you're ready. We'll eat first and then talk.'

'Ok. I'm pleased to meet you Kate.'

Sarah was intrigued. When she reached the table and sat down with her veggie curry and wild rice, Kate was just tucking into her beef hotpot. They made small talk as they ate and brought coffees back to the table when they had finished.

'First of all, Sarah, I'd like to tell you how impressed I was by your speech. You certainly do look at things differently to most people and I find your passion inspiring. '

'Well, thank you for saying so, Kate. I do get a bit irate sometimes but I feel really frustrated that attitudes are changing so very slowly and there is still an enormous amount of prejudice about.'

'Yes, I know what you mean. My great grandmother was a suffragette so I share your frustrations that opportunities for women are still not on a par with those of men. I'm interested in what you think are the main problems.'

'Well, I appreciate that there've been huge improvements over recent years but we're still a long way from where we should be. I often wonder if we'll see true equality in my lifetime. I was so naïve in 1975 when I thought things would change overnight.' They both smiled and nodded in agreement. 'I didn't allow for women themselves.'

'What do you mean by that?'

'Well, I hate to say it but I come across a lot of women who seem to be holding *themselves* back and putting *themselves* down.

Only a few weeks ago, I heard a young girl at my bank comment about expecting an office full of women to put up a heavy poster and why didn't the company send a man down to do it. I couldn't believe it! Of course I had to tackle her about it and told her she was a capable enough young woman and just to get on with it, ask for help if she needed it and stop being so lazy. She managed perfectly well.'

'Yes, I've noticed girls say they can't do something just to get out of doing it but it's not only girls that try that one'

'True. My friend's husband says he's no good at the washing up and his wife is much better at it. I told him he just needs more practice.' They both chuckled and felt the first warmth of a promising new friendship.

'I worry a bit about these younger women. I see too many that just don't want to fulfil their potential and would rather obsess over their looks all day instead. Don't misunderstand me. There's nothing wrong with trying to look your best but things are really getting out of hand. One girl told me she spent a hundred pounds on a tube of lip cream. I was stunned! I told her she should have more sense and truly her lips looked no better for it.'

'I know what you mean, Sarah. It used to be just celebrities that had implants here and reductions there but I know of several women, not very financially well off, who have saved up to have enhancements done.'

'Me too. It's getting terrible. I think they should be referred to psychiatrists first, to find out why they are so unhappy with their own image. They seem more obsessed with improving their looks than improving their brains. I want to shake them and tell them to do something worthwhile with their lives so that they're too busy to be constantly looking in the mirror.'

'I think you would too, Sarah!!' Lady Catherine couldn't help feeling hopeful already. She really liked the woman seated opposite her. She was like a kindred spirit. Perhaps at last................

She continued 'I've been campaigning for a long time against women's magazines that are making matters worse; they air brush pictures to make the women look impossibly perfect. They don't care about the damage they are doing to impressionable young girls. We need magazines to show celebrities as they really are and show the true beauty of women of all shapes and sizes. This is the real world.'

'Yes, but we also need our women to be strong enough to think for themselves and not fall into these traps. I have three grown up daughters who, I am proud to say, are very strong women. Of course this made their teen years very interesting' she grimaced 'but I wanted them to challenge me and form their own opinions. I know I can be a bit of a control freak! '

Sarah couldn't believe how easy it was talking to this intelligent older woman and she felt no inhibitions about showing her true nature, warts and all.

'Do you have any children, Kate?'

'No, unfortunately not. We tried for many years but it just wasn't to be. It's always been a deep regret for both of us'

'Oh, I am so sorry. As much trouble as mine have given me over the years, I wouldn't be without them'

'We have made SOME strides forward though, don't you think Sarah? We have women pilots and judges and soldiers that fight alongside the men in the armed forces. There are many women, like myself, that run businesses.'

'Oh definitely, some jobs are now far more accessible to women but it's been nearly thirty years so ALL jobs should be. By now we should expect to see a good balance of men and women in all occupations to reflect the population, not just token women here and there. Now, is this problem the lack of opportunity or the lack of will from the women? Perhaps it's a bit of both.'

'Yes, perhaps'

They both fell silent as they finished their drinks.

'I remember before I had the children. I wasn't very happy at work and saw another bank job advertised and applied for it. The man interviewing me was more interested in when I would start a family than my ability to do the job. He said I would be tied down by family and couldn't move to a different branch if they needed me to. I asked him if he would say the same to a man but he didn't reply. Of course I didn't get the job.

I settled into my old role a bit more and stopped looking at vacancies but a few months later I received a letter from the Equal Opportunities office. Someone else had complained about the interviewer's attitude and they wanted details of my experience. It led to that bank getting a huge fine. I think it was one of the first major cases of its kind'

'Excellent.......sometimes the letter of the law really does work'

'Yes but often it can be got around in practice. Although I've been one of the first generation of women to have it all, a family and career, (which is why I always look so exhausted!), I still think women that chose to solely care for their children should be more valued than they are. It should be her choice but she should be given much more help to return to her career when she's ready. But even now I still hear women managers as well as the men, give preference to staff without children or who're unlikely to go on maternity leave.'

'That's incredible'. Kate was beginning to understand what Sarah meant about women themselves being part of the problem.

'Of course men in blue collar jobs can still be far worse. About two years ago, my husband employed a young woman as an engineering apprentice. After the interviews, when he was making his decision, other managers were telling him he couldn't employ a woman as it would distract the men (bless their weak souls!) and there weren't enough toilet facilities, except over in the office block.

I asked him if he thought she was the best candidate and he said yes. It was between her and another man but she was more enthusiastic and interviewed better and the man seemed bored and disinterested and was already in a higher paid job. I told him he had to employ her then or he'd be breaking the law otherwise. Thankfully he had already decided to do so, but I expect lots of other men in his place would have caved in to his colleagues.

She's turned out to be one of the better more reliable engineers they've had and she fitted right in with the rest of the staff straight away with her bubbly personality and open friendliness. And why wouldn't she?' They both nodded and went into their own thoughts for a minute.

They decided they had time to fetch more coffees and brought them back to their table.

10 SARAH'S DREAM

'You deal with people at the bank all the time, Sarah. Do you still see younger people with old fashioned attitudes to women or is it just in the older generations?'

'Well, some elderly gents still prefer to speak to a man about their business and my office is mostly women at the moment so they have had to get used to us. We treat them gently! But very occasionally you get someone younger who really should know better.

I came across a man the other week who was right out of the 1950's. He came in to the office to open a new account for his son and for himself. His son was going to university in a couple of year's time so they both wanted to save up.

It transpired that the boy had a younger sister so of course I commented that the earlier you start saving, the better, particularly if you had two children to put through university. He told me he wasn't going to waste money on sending his daughter to university, as she would only get married and have children! He said it was much more important for a man to have a good career! Can you believe it? This IS the 21st century isn't it?'

'I'm astonished that someone can still have that sort of attitude'

'I pointed out to him, much more politely than I felt like doing, that men get married and have children too and it's just as important for a girl to get a good education so that she can also have a good career.

'Look around this office.' I said to him 'Every one of the women in here, except one young girl on the counter, is married with children. That includes the branch manager and, when I come to think about it, the area manager as well.'

I don't think he cared. I felt very sorry for his daughter, but also for his son, who had to listen to all this. It's more than likely that he'll adopt the same outdated attitude unless he meets some strong women at university who change his mind. I said goodbye and watched them struggle to get back into their time machine, ha!!'

They both laughed, knowing it was more sad than funny.

'Well, Sarah. What would YOU do to try and change things, if you had all the money in the world?'

She didn't have to think for long.

'Please don't laugh, Kate, but I have always dreamed of opening a school, but not just for girls. I feel it's important that boys are also taught to have respect for others regardless of gender.'

'That's interesting. Tell me more'

'This sounds crazy………'

'No please, go on'

'Ok…….It would be by invitation only and would be free to attend. I would definitely consider inviting the boy and girl from the time machine! Students would be able to stay at the school until they finished their whole education so we would offer graduate and post graduate courses.

I would want to produce well rounded, ambitious adults that are capable of going onto whatever career they desired, hopefully in positions where they'd have some influence to change things for the better. Their skills would be much sort after by employers and governments around the world so perhaps they could help with funding.

It wouldn't be an ordinary school. I would want to teach things like martial arts, survival skills, and some of the more useful languages. Anything that would be vital in the world we find ourselves in today. I would bring in new subjects if necessary, tailored to the skills of individual pupils.

I would also like a state of the art science and technology unit that would lead the way in the search for a cheap clean carbon free fuel and would produce cutting edge technology that would only be limited by our imaginations.

Hopefully, in time, my pupils would be in all walks of life. They'd be confident and skilful and always have empathy and respect for others but would be encouraged to challenge unfairness in all forms. Hopefully they'd prove to be excellent role models for those around them and we could then at last change the craziness once and for all.

Right, Kate. I've finished idealising now. I'll shut up.'

They both smiled at each other.

'I find what you've said very interesting, Sarah. What if I told you that I could help you make this dream come true?'

11 AN INCREDIBLE PROPOSAL

'I'd wonder what you had been slipping into your coffee while I wasn't looking!' they both laughed.

'How much do you think it would cost to set up and run such a school?'

'I've no idea. I haven't got that far. I could never come up with that sort of money so it is really only a pipe dream.'

'How would you feel if I could offer you a house in the middle of nowhere with extensive grounds and hundreds of millions of pounds to put to good use'

'Again, I'd wonder what you've been slipping into your coffee.'

'I'm serious Sarah. I have an old estate that I inherited from a great uncle who I hardly knew. He also left me his huge fortune and I have no need of either the estate or the money. The house needs totally refurbishing but I have been looking for a worthwhile use for it for many years and have struggled to find something suitable. I had given up looking until today, when I heard your speech and we had this chat.

As I said, my great grandmother was a suffragette and I can't help thinking that it was fate that brought us together today. I want to make a difference with my uncle's money and I am willing to allow you to use it to set up the school and run it for as long as you need.

I have made many contacts through my own business and also my husband's and through my seat in the House of Lords. If you would allow me to, I would like to help by being responsible for getting ongoing funding.'

'I can't quite take this in. Why would you do this for me, when we hardly know each other?'

'I'm a pretty good judge of people and this is not just for you, don't forget. It's for generations to come.'

'OK…..It looks like it's time we went back to our seats now. Not that I will be able to concentrate for the rest of the day'

'Perhaps we can meet at my home one day next week and we can talk about things further'

'Yes, that would be good.' They exchanged business cards.

'I'll call you to arrange a suitable time. I am so glad that we met today, Sarah. This means a lot to me'

'Me too, except I am sure I will find that I have fallen asleep in the conference hall and this has all been a dream'

They shook hands and made their way back to their seats for the afternoon session.

12 REVELATIONS AT TRESCOTHAM HALL

'I'm not surprised Mum's involved', said Kim, 'I just can't believe she kept it from us for all these years. I knew she'd left the bank and was working from home but I thought she owned a mortgage brokerage. Why wouldn't she tell us she had her own school?'

'As I said, the school she initially envisaged is totally different to the school we have today. Events were brought to light that meant her plans for the school HAD to change and made security and therefore secrecy, so essential'

'But ten years!! She kept it from us for ten years!!' Molly could see how upset her mum was and that she wasn't taking in what Beth Drake was saying.

'Please, Mum, just listen to Ms Drake. I'm sure she'll explain everything if you give her a chance.'

'Ok, sorry, Beth, please go on.'

'I am aware this has been very upsetting for you but there is a very good reason why Sarah could not tell you about the school. Let me explain further.

Of course it takes time to set up a school from scratch and there were major refurbishments needed to Trescotham Hall. Money was not an issue as Sarah had the financial backing of Lady Catherine Sampson who owns the estate.

They were almost ready to start thinking about suitable staff and which children would be given the first invitations, when Sarah was called to a meeting at Lady Catherine's home. There were several people there, top scientists and politicians but most notable was the Prime Minister himself.

It was explained to Sarah that they had discovered a strange phenomenon and they needed her help. Several young girls aged around ten and eleven had developed enhanced abilities. At that time they weren't sure how long this had been going on'

Mark, Kim and Molly, looked from one to another.

'These enhancements included improved vision, hearing, memory, speed, amongst others. They didn't seem to be born that way but rather they developed, almost overnight.

Naturally their parents were extremely worried and the girls themselves had difficulty coping with the changes that were happening to them.

The country's top scientists were brought in to investigate but it soon became apparent that it was not just confined to the UK. Other countries were discovering that some of their girls were experiencing the same changes.

The politicians and scientists from each country got together and decided to pool their knowledge so that they could find out what was going on much more quickly. They decided that until they had some answers the whole thing must be kept secret in order to protect the girls'

'That's why we haven't heard anything in the news then, although I remember a few years ago a girl who was supposed to have remarkable vision', said Mark.

'Yes, sometimes news stories leak out before the girls' parents can be contacted but luckily I don't think people take those sorts of stories too seriously, thank goodness.

Well, it took quite a while to come up with a theory of what was happening.

The first major concern was that these girls had been genetically manipulated somehow by someone, for their own gain, but thankfully that was quickly ruled out. It was established that it was only girls that were affected as there was no evidence of these enhanced abilities in any boys so far, but of course, this could still happen.

Eventually it was concluded that it was some sort of evolutionary process. To put it very simply, we naturally evolve as a species and the skills that help us survive are passed to the next generation who enhance them further and pass those, in turn, to their offspring. Sometimes there are anomalies called 'mutations' that bring diversity and gradual change over many, many generations.'

Kim, Mark & Molly all nodded that they understood.

'Yes, I remember going on a school trip years ago to a Victorian House. The beds were really small and their shoes were tiny in comparison to nowadays and that's only a few generations back' said Kim.

'I remember the teacher saying we are generally much taller and have much larger feet than our ancestors; partly due to our healthier diets. Unfortunately we are also getting much fatter due to too much fast food and not having to work physically hard to put food on the table. We can reverse the weight issue though with better education and more exercise.

We all love to watch the documentary channels so we've seen lots of programmes on Darwin's theories of evolution so we do understand so far.'

'Excellent. Well, it's thought that these girls have 'jumped', for want of a better word, some stages of evolution and have abilities that the rest of us will take a lot longer to achieve. It is suspected that Mother Nature has just given the girls a much needed leg up, so to speak.'

'So where did Mum come into all this?'

'The Prime Minister at the time personally asked Sarah if she would consider running the school purely for these special girls. He wanted to give them a safe environment in which to continue their education, with other girls who were going through the same thing.

He also wanted the girls to be trained for top ranking jobs where their skills could be put to good use, but he wanted Sarah and her staff to act as a moral buffer so that neither he, nor any future Prime Minister or government could take advantage of any of the girls against their will. It was a big responsibility for her to take on and it was also unchartered waters for everyone concerned.

They also discussed the global implications. Other nations were making the right noises so far, but eventually they may not be so scrupulous where their own girls were concerned. There was a real possibility that they could be transformed into a formidable mini army that would threaten the security of the UK. The Prime Minister wanted her to bear this in mind when she got as far as setting up the school curriculum.'

'So this is a girls-only school and all the pupils have enhanced abilities?'

'Yes, Kim, but the girls call them 'Ants'. I think it gradually got shortened from 'enhancements'. We work with the girls, not only on their basic education but also on helping them to understand and control their Ants and we have even managed to develop them further.'

'But surely you don't think Molly is one of these girls, yet why would you have invited us here today if not? I think you've made a mistake. Molly is just a bit above average at school. We know there's something unusual about her sometimes, but not this,' her father looked very worried.

'I think it's time for Molly to get everything out in the open now'

13 MOLLY HAS ANTS

'OK, Molly, there's nothing to worry about'

Beth moved over to sit beside her, took both of her hands in hers and looked deep into her eyes.

'Molly, I know you have been hiding what you are really capable of from your family, but now is the time to let it all out into the open. I must tell you that I fully understand what you are going through because I'm the same as you, as I think you already suspect. I was one of the very first that we know of. That is one of the reasons your grandmother eventually chose me as the school principle. I was in my early 20's by the time I first met her and had just qualified as a teacher.'

Molly looked at both of her parents with tears in her eyes. Her voice showed she was full of barely reigned in emotion when she said,

'I'm sorry I've kept things hidden. I never wanted you to think of me as a freak' she said to her parents.

Mark & Kim rushed over to comfort her as Beth moved away.

'We'd NEVER think that! We've always known you were special in some ways. Don't ever think we'd think less of you. Beth, I don't understand. I thought you said the girls developed their abilities at age 10 or 11. As far as I can tell Molly has been like this since she was born.'

'Yes, we are aware of that. Of course, Sarah and I both know what to look out for, even though all of the gifted girls are extremely good at hiding what they can do. However we do think Molly may be the first one to have had the abilities from birth. Still, Sarah felt she didn't want to introduce Molly to the school too early. to give her the chance to try a 'normal' childhood first, but she has been keeping a close eye on her, all the same.

Ok Molly. Just take your time and tell us what you think you can do that others can't do as well. We'll try not to interrupt you, just tell us everything. We know what a relief it will be for you'

Molly had a quick drink of her juice and Kim's heart nearly broke at her trembling hand.

'Right...............I'll start with my sight. I can see a very long way. I don't know how far but VERY far. I can see minute detail. I can easily read a car number plate on the road from here, which is six miles away, as long as there are no hills in the way, but I can see much further, right into space if I look up. I can also see very close up, almost like looking through a microscope but I can choose how I want to see things and how far I want to see.' She paused before continuing further. This wasn't as hard as she'd thought it would be. The weight she didn't realise she had been carrying, gradually began lifting from her shoulders.

'I can hear things from miles away. Again, I've not sure of my limits, and I can hear the quietest of sounds as well. I've learnt to filter what I can hear though so I can make sense of it.' She gave a wry smile. 'I know you both had an idea I had better than average hearing especially when you want to talk in private; I've heard you say to wait until I was asleep.' Her parents nodded agreement but didn't interrupt.

'I can read what people are thinking. It's not as clear as the actual words like 'I....like.....that.....picture', so it's not exactly 'mind reading'. It's more of a sense or feeling that that person likes that picture. I have to really concentrate though. If there are a lot of distractions, I lose the connection. I can read their emotions too, so I can tell if someone is afraid or nervous even if they aren't showing it on the outside and I almost feel it myself.

It's not just people I can read either. I can understand what animals are trying to communicate and can get across to them somehow too. Not using any words, it's just an awareness. I'll show you.' She went over to the window.

'That bird chirping outside on the window ledge is cross because she's seen a big juicy worm that she wants to feed to her babies back in the nest, but there's a big tabby cat sitting close by who's showing no signs of budging. I'll get the cat to move round to the other side of the house.'

To the others, it just looked like Molly was gazing out of the window deep in thought. They all got up to see what was happening outside.

The tabby lazily stretched, then slowly rose from her warm spot under the bushes and took a very regal walk toward the other side of the house. The bird swooped down and plucked the worm from the damp soil and flew out of sight.

'I deliberately avoided reading the worm' she gave a wry smile 'but the bird was very grateful.'

14 MORE ANTS

'You're right, Ms Drake, it is a relief to get things out in the open at last. I hadn't realised how difficult it's been to keep everything to myself.' It was Beth Drakes turn to smile assurance.

'OK.........next. I have an eidetic memory. That means 'Photographic', Mum. I've never forgotten anything I've read or done or seen but I've pretended to, especially at school. I don't want to stand out from the others and be ridiculed; It's hard enough. It's like at sport's day. I can run faster than anyone else I know, but I always make sure I come in second to be on the safe side.' The way she said this, so matter-of-factly, amused her listeners.

'Something else I can do that I only recently discovered is that I can understand any language after hearing just a few words. That one is really weird. I discovered it last term when we got a new teacher, who's from France. I heard her talking in French and suddenly I could understand her. Before I could stop myself I was speaking fluently to her with a perfect accent. I had to tell her a little white lie and said we had been going to France for our holidays since I was small and that I was forgetting how to speak it as we hadn't been for a couple of years. Sorry, Mum. I could sense she was not suspicious of me at all and was quite happy with my explanation.

It's not just spoken language I can understand either. I can understand mathematical equations and I'm great at codes and puzzles but mostly the thing I enjoy is computer code. I can understand and write computer code. I am certain I can hack any computer in the world, quite easily. Don't worry' she quickly went on. 'I haven't tried it......yet.

Another quite weird thing I can do. Do you remember, Mum, you're always saying that my cousin Julie must emit an electrical aura because every computer or printer or any other electronic device she touches, ends up breaking for no apparent reason?'

' I don't really think that, it's just that all her gadgets *do* break down on her all the time and her work has banned her from going near some of their vital equipment'

'I know, ha! Well I can do it for real without breaking anything. If I really concentrate hard and place my hand over a computer or keyboard or anything electronic, I can feel a heat flow from my hand and I can……….interface? I'm not sure that is the right word to explain it, but I can make the necessary contacts to complete circuits by using that heat and my mind. I just instinctively know what to do to get the device to do what I want. I've no idea how.' They listened intently. Mark wanted to jump in with questions but they had agreed not to interrupt.

'Right…. Another thing I can do is tell when people are ill, even if they don't know yet. Again, I can turn this on or off so I don't go around sensing every ill person, but when I try, I can see small areas on them that 'glow' for want of a better word. It's only very faint, almost just a shimmer and I get a strange sweet smell from them.

I knew one of the teachers had a bad appendix once. I chickened out of telling him and got another student to say he didn't look well and ought to go to the doctors, which he did and he was taken straight into hospital.

On the other hand I'm a very quick healer myself. This I HAVEN'T been able to hide so Mum & Dad know this. Luckily I've only had a few scrapes so far. I always dreaded breaking a bone or something more serious. I thought it would definitely raise the freak meter a few notches if I did'

'Now Molly, You must stop thinking of yourself as a freak. Your insulting me as well you know.'

'Sorry, Miss Drake but it's how I've always thought of myself so it's very difficult to think otherwise'

'I'm sure *we* can help you there. Now is that everything so far.'

'Yes, I'm quite sure I haven't forgotten anything!' they laughed which felt good to them all.

'I am always conscious of the fact that I may have an ability that I haven't yet had to use though.'

'Well, before I come to that and explain about the other girls at the school and how the school can help you, I'm sure your parents have lots of questions for you first. It has been such a shock for you all today'

15 FAMILY CHAT

Her parents were seated on either side, each with an arm around her and both started talking at the same time.

'Mum, Dad, just give me a chance to answer one question before you ask me another'

'Sorry sweetheart, we just want you to know how much we still love you and nothing will ever change that. We're so proud of how you have handled yourself so far and we want you to know you no longer have to carry this secret around on your own'

'Thanks Dad'

'Have you ever mentioned anything to Nan or the boys?'

'Not to Nan but I could tell she knew. I just didn't know how much. I got the feeling she was being very patient, waiting for me to tell her first. I find it MUCH harder to read close relatives than strangers though.'

'That's good!'

'The boys know more than you but not everything. They tease me all the time but I suppose that is a little brother thing. They call it my 'Mojo Thing' 'Do your Mojo Thing to that girl to see if she fancies me' that was Lucas, the other day! The funny thing is, I've never once needed to tell them not to tell anyone. It's as if they instinctively know that to let on would be bad. They just accept me as I am though. Their weird sister, ha!'

'What about your teachers? Do any of them suspect anything or give you a hard time'

'No, not really. I can tell sometimes when a thought crosses a teachers mind, say, if I remember a bit too much, but I just forget a few things or look like I'm trying hard to remember and it goes away.'

'My mind's still in a whirl, sweetheart, but I'm sure we'll have lots of time to come up with more questions when we get home. I'd like to know more from you please Beth, about why exactly we are here. My Mum could have told us all this so far.'

'Ok Kim. Sarah wanted ME to tell you for Molly's sake. She felt it would be much easier for her to reveal everything about her true abilities to someone with abilities herself. And it is often easier to talk to strangers but she felt Molly still needed you both here for support and you needed to hear what she had to say. She thought it better that you came to the school for this meeting so that there were no distractions by the boys.

She also wanted me to show you all around the school and if you like what you see, I am to extend a formal invitation for Molly to attend as a student'

Molly's face lit up.

'You did say there were no fees?' Beth nodded. 'But what if we don't like what we see?'

'Well, Mark, you are perfectly free to take Molly home and educate her any way you choose. All I ask is that you never discuss anything about today, including the location or even the existence of the school, with anyone ever, except Sarah of course. For all our sakes.'

Kim & Mark nodded agreement.

'Now, most of our girls (and myself of course) have similar Ants to varying degrees so I think you have at least one other that you may not be aware of, Molly. Have you tried to see how long you can stay under water?'

'No, I've never tried it.'

'Well, all of our girls can breathe underwater, some for as long as an hour. Their bodies seem to adapt to breathing the much lower oxygen content in the water, for a short time but not indefinitely.

However, I think you have a few Ants that we don't. I'm not aware that any of our students can use their hands to manipulate electronics the way that you can. I think your instant language skills, your way with animals and the way you can see and smell illness are all unique to you too. So we will of course be interested particularly in those Ants.

I must stress at this point though, that our girls are in no way treated like lab rats to experiment on. No girl will be pressured into doing anything she doesn't want to, but the girls are intelligent enough to want to understand their Ants as much as we do.

Something else. It is thought that all the girls have an extended life expectancy, maybe as long as two hundred and fifty years but of course we can't prove that just yet. It doesn't mean immortality, Molly, so don't start doing anything dangerous! It just means the girls age much more slowly.

Ok. Are you ready to take the tour? We'll take a walk over to the woods first, if you're up to it. We won't

stay outside long in this cold but it will certainly clear
the cobwebs away.'

16 THE TOUR BEGINS

Beth continued to explain a little more about the origins of the school as they walked briskly along, trying to keep warm.

'Of course in the beginning we were all feeling our way and we did have a few teething problems. Our first big mistake was in our choice of teaching staff. Candidates had been lined up before Sarah knew about the girls and I was one of those candidates.

I hadn't declared my own abilities on the original application of course and even when I finally had my interview and was told about the unusual students we were now expecting, I still kept quiet. I think it was just a habit I'd developed over the years, to keep my Ants to myself. I suppose it's self preservation really.' She smiled at Molly.

However, I was concerned as I knew I wouldn't be able to keep my secret from the girls but I was also thrilled as suddenly I was no longer alone. And yes, Molly, I too had felt like a freak'

'It quickly became clear that the 'normal' teachers, (the girls call non-enhanced people 'Norms' by the way. A nickname for everything!) the Norms were struggling to cope. These were the top teachers in their profession but they had the mental capacity of newborns compared to the geniuses they were expected to educate. We totally underestimated the IQ of our girls.

A new school board had been created by then and Sarah called a meeting at Lady Catherine's, to brainstorm the problem. Sarah is very astute and she was starting to suspect that I had Ants even though I'd played them down. I was the only teacher not having any trouble with my students and we were even starting to begin to trust one another.

It was decided to give the existing teaching staff extremely generous termination bonuses and a yearly allowance which would stop if they ever spoke about the girls to anyone. New positions were to be found for them too.

I was to be offered the job of Principle and would take complete control over all running of the school, including the domestics, setting of the curriculum and hiring of the new staff. I was to be answerable only to Sarah who would arrange for adequate funds to be at my disposal and would help me with any decision making.

So, I think I've brought you up to date with the background of the school now. It has been extremely hard work but very enjoyable and I haven't always got things right either. Our teaching staff over the years have had some of the brightest minds from around the world and although the students still had much higher IQ's, they still had a lot to learn from each other. Now all of our teachers are ex pupils so our teaching standards are the very highest they can be. Our curriculum is rather unusual too, as you will soon see.

Many of our girls have graduated and gone on to their various careers. They all still have a deep affection for the school though, even after they leave. They treat it as if it's a much-loved home that they have to protect and can't wait to get back to, whenever they can. All of them keep in touch and update us on how they are doing and of course, we're ALWAYS here for them should they need any help from US.'

'What sorts of jobs are they doing?'

'Well, Mark, we have several alumni in the secret services, MI5 & MI6, also Scotland Yard, SOCA the Serious Organised Crime Agency, Interpol, amongst others. Not just in law enforcement but we have top scientist working in forensics as well as research, medicine and social economics. They work at NASA, Microsoft and Apple and many corporations both very large and very small, well known and not so well known. We have several ex students in the Army, Navy, Air force and the Coastguard as well as in air, sea rescue. We have two in government….'

'Oo, which two, let me guess….'

'Sorry, Kim. We naturally keep the details of our placements confidential to protect us all.'

'Of course, sorry, I was getting a bit carried away there'

'Do they all have such high profile work?'

'Not if they don't want to. It is the student's own choice. We just make it easier for them to enter these sorts of professions if that is their preferred career. We have some students who have chosen instead to become musicians, artists, thespians, authors of both fiction and non-fiction. I suppose they chose to enrich lives rather than protect them, which is equally as important.

If they chose to do nothing at all, that would be such a waste but totally up to the student. However, I think their highly developed intelligence would make this most unlikely. Here we are at the first area that I want to show you'

17 SURVIVAL

'This is where our initial survival training takes place. We are just on the very edge of the area as it stretches for approximately twenty square miles. The girls are brought out here in all types of weather conditions and have to survive with what they have with them for a minimum of four weeks. The record so far is ten weeks.

Don't look so worried, we give them all the skills they need and we keep a close eye on them in case of emergencies. And don't forget, these are not your everyday tweenagers. We haven't had anyone starve to death or die just yet'

'Sounds horrendous to me!'

'You couldn't do without your home comforts Mum. Sounds fantastic to me, I can't wait!'

'We haven't made any decisions about sending you here yet, Molls. We need to see a lot more first'

'I know Dad, but you are feeling quite positive so far'

Mark frowned at being so transparent to his daughter, although of course he always had been but didn't realise it. It crossed his mind that family was supposed to be more difficult for her. Not impossible though obviously.

'As the girls advance we also take them to various other terrains around the world to teach them to survive anywhere under any conditions. We have sites in places such as the Arctic, Antarctic, the Sahara, the Himalayas, the Amazon rain forest.

Please let me know if you have any questions about anything you see. I will tell you as much as I am able to for security reasons'

'It's like 'I'm a Celebrity, Get Me Outta Here' for kids'

'No, I assure you Kim, it's much tougher than that and a lot more useful to the girls.

Ok, let's get back inside. You two look like you're feeling the cold a bit now. There are a few more large areas several miles away from the main school. The girls, of course jog over but we have golf buggies available for guests and visitors. I will explain those areas to you later in the tour but I think you will agree there is no need to go over there today as it's so cold. We'll head over to the Aqua Centre next'

18 THE TOUR CONTINUES

'This is one of my favourite areas of the school. We had this huge extension added, not long after the school opened, when we realised about the underwater breathing Ants. Like you Molly, I didn't realise I had them myself until we discovered them in other students.

We, of course had a swimming pool with a state of the art Spa for both exercise and relaxation but we also now have a few extras. I know some of the classes may sound unnecessary to you after what we've discussed but the girls can't stay underwater indefinitely. They certainly don't want to raise any suspicions in the outside world, so they not only have to be able to USE the equipment but also have to learn to PRETEND to use it.

We have a dive tank where they can learn to use equipment such as rebreathers for example. As the name suggests, these are light weight breathing kits that recycle some of the air that you breathe out. We also have a Disaster Recovery Pool (DRP) where we can set up scenarios, such as a vehicle plummeting into a lake, so that the girls can learn how best to respond.

They are of course taught all aspects of first aid including resuscitation techniques. Once the students are proficient in the DRP they get chance to practice in our lake where visibility is not as good and where nature can intervene at any time. We don't only do this in summer of course. Disasters don't take a note of the weather before they happen.'

'The only bit I fancy is the Spa! I could do with a nice massage and a soak in the hot tub at this minute. You can't beat a bit of pampering!'

'I'm sure that could be arranged Kim, if you have time after our tour'

'Wow, really? I wasn't serious but if it's OK....'

'Mum, you're so embarrassing!'

'Don't worry, Molly, I'm sure you would all enjoy an hour in the Spa before your journey home. Dad, too. It's there for all staff and visitors to use as well as the students.

We have a separate Martial Arts studio next door where we teach all types of disciplines and even hand to hand combat. We also have an excellent gym where we help the girls develop their physical Ants. It's right next to the Aqua Centre and has a full size running track as well as all the equipment you could ever need, if any of you are feeling energetic instead. Mark?'

'I think I'm with Kim on this one. The Spa it is!'

They all chuckled.

'Let's move on. As you can see, this whole quadrangle is dedicated to classrooms. The students are responsible for tending the gardens in the centre. This half is very peaceful to sit in in the summer as they have made a secret garden in the centre which can't be seen from here. The smells from the plants are wonderful and very soothing.

On the far side is the vegetable garden. We grow enough to feed the school, not only to make us self sufficient but also to teach useful skills and give the students a feeling of satisfaction. We also have another small plot, near the science wing, where we test-grow plants for medicine and a large field, well away from here where our science classes are trying to help with the age old problem of feeding the world safely and cheaply. They have already discovered a very cheap and easy way of making filthy, polluted water into drinking water, that is changing the lives of so many people in under developed countries. We are so proud of them.'

'I read about that in the papers. Children came up with that?'

'Yes, Mark, but children with Ants, don't forget.

In these classrooms we teach the basic subjects of Maths, English, Science, History and Geography, which everyone must attend. We also teach many other subjects like Philosophy, Art, Music, which the students have requested. This part of the curriculum is very fluid, depending on the students we have here at the time'

'Yuk, I thought I might get away from having to do History and Geography'

'No, sorry Molly. It's important that NO element of your basic education is overlooked. We do start at the basics in case there are any gaps in a child's knowledge from before they first arrive here, as they come from so many varied backgrounds. As you can imagine though, progress is extremely fast and they are soon onto more advanced studies of these subjects.'

'But why are all the classrooms empty, I thought the Aqua Centre might not be being used as they were all in class. We don't seem to have seen any of the girls yet'

'My apologies, Kim, I should have told you that most of them are away from school with some due back on Sunday evening'

'Of course, it's half term. I'd forgotten'

'No, not really. We don't have set terms as at your children's school. Still, we are extremely flexible with time off for our students but as this is a particularly quiet week with so many girls off training abroad at the same time, some of the pupils have taken the opportunity to go home for a short break.

Although they are free to go home every weekend if they so wish and if it is practical for them to do so, they do tend to get caught up in activities at the weekends, which they struggle to tear themselves away from, so be warned!

They are also allowed 12 weeks holiday from school per year each to be taken whenever they wish. The school never closes. There are some pupils still here, doing various activities but we haven't come across them yet. I am certain they know exactly where we are though!

As I mentioned earlier, we teach many varied languages. These classrooms we are coming to now, all have sound booths inside them to help the children immerse themselves in the language to help with understanding and speaking in different dialects. You may still find our language suite useful, Molly, despite your Ant. We also send students to live with native families for a while so that they can learn more about their culture, first hand, all in a safe environment.

All of the rooms on the far side of the quadrangle are our computer sciences suite where all the girls hone their computer programming skills but mainly those who specialise in the subject work on their many varied projects in there. The remaining classrooms cater for the rest of the academic subjects.

Now, lets go over to the science wing'

19 CLEVER INVENTIONS

'This is our experimental garden that I mentioned earlier where we test grow plants that we have manipulated in the lab, mostly these are for medical use. We also have a large field in an isolated part of the grounds which is divided into sections where we test grow different food crops'

'Are you sure these are safe to use? It all sounds a bit like a bad 1950's Sci Fi movie to me'

'I assure you Mark, every precaution is taken to make sure all our plants are protected from getting into the normal food chain, until we have thoroughly tested them and passed them as safe. In fact our procedures are so tight, they are now being adopted around the world by other such laboratories.'

'So these plants are used for medicines? I know a lot of our drugs today are based on plants that have been used for centuries but I take it you are experimenting with new plants?'

'Yes, we have plant seeds sent to us from all corners of the globe and we now have the largest collection in the world. We think there are many yet to be discovered, in remote places where it is difficult for humans to get to, so we do some amazing field trips looking for them!! Is this an area you think you may be interested in Molly?'

'Perhaps, but I think I'm more interested in how things work, like engines and computers and things. I think I'd be much happier looking like a crazy inventor designing some new contraption. This stuff still interests me though. Have you come up with any new medicines yet?'

'Yes, quite a number over the years, some of which are now taken for granted, like sugar control tablets for diabetics and tablets to control cholesterol. We have two major drugs trials coming to an end, with incredible results so far, which we are very excited about.

The two drugs are based on one single drug which has been developed to solve two opposite problems. One will make obesity a thing of the past and the other will make starvation a thing of the past. So both the developed and developing worlds will benefit. We are hoping the drugs will be available towards the end of next year'

'Wow, that sounds amazing!! I've longed for a decent diet pill for years but surely the pill to stop you starving is no substitute for food?'

'No, of course they are not meant to replace food indefinitely but they will be offered free to the aid agencies who will arrange for them to get to the right people, along with the tablets that clean dirty water for drinking. They are safe to use on children and babies and we hope they will save many, many lives until any food crisis is resolved.

The 'diet' pills as you called them, Kim, don't work like existing pills on the market that just make you feel full. These process your food more efficiently so that you can still enjoy eating whatever you want but your body will go to a more natural weight and stay there. In practice, as we had hoped, you won't want to just sit and eat a mountain of food and do no exercise, as the speedier process actually gives you more energy. Our trial subjects have all toned up their bodies considerably through doing more exercise, which they actually felt like doing and have enjoyed.'

'Sounds fantastic!! Put me down for some'

'We are hoping they will be able to be sold over the counter as we have eliminated all side effects, so they will be even safer than buying aspirin'

'Heaven'

'If you'd like to step through here you will see our labs are extremely well equipped. There should be some girls about here somewhere who have stayed at school to finish our most important current project. I heard them working earlier......ah here they are'

20 FIRST CONTACT

'Molly, this is Phoebe and Freya, two of our students. Girls, this is Molly, who is having our guided tour with a view to perhaps joining us here at Trescotham Hall.'

Phoebe had the most beautiful long red hair that Molly had ever seen. It was totally different to Beth Drake's shade. It was more like a dark rich rose gold colour which caught the light whenever she moved. It was tending to curl towards the ends and looked like it was being barely tamed by the chunky clip she had in place, but Molly still envied her those long tresses. She had big brown eyes, an unusual combination with red hair, (but Ms Drake had this combination too), and she was taller than Molly with a slightly more slender build.

Freya, couldn't have been more different. She had short cropped and choppy, extremely dark, almost black, hair. She was much taller than the other two girls and had a build like the mythical Amazonian warrior. She had, what Molly called, 'see through eyes'. Very, very pale blue that seemed to almost disappear and which had always unnerved her. She had never felt the urge to look very deep into anyone's eyes to see what she could see there. However she felt nothing but warmth and good feelings coming from both of these girls as they all greeted each other.

'Why don't you show Molly your project and take her around the rest of the science wing and I'll take her parents round and meet you back here in about half an hour?'

The girls escorted Molly to the room they had been heading back to. It looked like something from CSI Crime Scene Investigation from the telly. It had all the usual lab equipment but some that looked extremely high tech. There were images that looked to be floating in mid air, which showed various computer desktops and open screens. Phoebe waved her arms in the air and the screens moved in front of them into a stack that looked like paper files on a desk. Molly was just thrilled.

'Have you met any of the other girls yet'

'No, you're the first girls I've ever met that are like me, apart from Ms Drake, who isn't a girl of course........' Molly couldn't help feeling nervous at this first encounter.

'There's no need to be nervous Molly. You're amongst friends here. We all develop a deep understanding of each other and a strong bond, in time, and you'll make some lifelong alliances. It's very difficult in the beginning though. I remember it well!' Phoebe's laugh was just as pretty as she was.

'Yes, Phoebe arrived several weeks before I did. She was still finding it difficult to be herself and was still keeping her full Ants hidden but I didn't have the same trouble. I found it such a relief to let everything go and trusted everyone here right away. I helped Phoebe to see that she could do the same and we have been best buds ever since.'

'Today has been such a shocking, yet fantastic day for me but I still can't believe that there are so many other girls like me about. I would be gutted if my parents wouldn't let me come here but thankfully I'm feeling that they're almost as thrilled about this place as I am.

What is the project you are working on? I sensed Ms Drake was extremely excited about it. Both of you are too'

'Yes, we have almost finished our final tests and are planning to launch it next week. We're sure it will be a huge benefit to everyone and will hopefully save us all from global warming.'

'Wow, saving the planet!'

'Not exactly, Molly. The planet isn't in any danger from us. It's had much more violent weather in its ancient history and survived, and it'll do so again. The climate constantly changes anyway and regardless, we may not all survive the next natural ice age in about 1500 years time.

It's just that we humans are changing the temperature artificially and very quickly. It's life on Earth that's in danger, not the planet itself.' Phoebe's brown eyes were bright with excitement as she warmed to her subject. Molly had never heard anyone of her age talk like this before. She loved it.

'The core of the problem is the burning of fossil fuels, but instead of dealing with that by changing the fuel we use, they try not to use as much of it and that isn't the answer. It's like treating the symptoms of an illness instead of dealing with the root cause.'

'Or telling you not to use plastic carrier bags instead of making them dissolvable. Are you supposed to put all your shopping in your pockets?' Freya joined in.

They all laughed. Phoebe was a natural orator and held them spellbound as she spoke, and Molly could tell Freya felt just as passionately.

'Makes sense to me, but when I've talked to my Dad about going green and why we still use oil he says we couldn't do without the oil companies as the world economy would collapse.'

'Well, not if the oil companies had invested in the new technology but they haven't had the vision to do so. They're even still drilling for fresh oil fields which shows the message about climate change still isn't getting through to them.

Tell your Dad not to worry about the economy though. New greener businesses will soon spring up so everything will be fine. The world will be in a much better healthier state without them and so will our chances of survival'

'You seem to know so much more than I do and yet you must be only a year or two older?'

'Don't worry Molly, you haven't had your Ants developed yet like Phoebe and I and the rest of us here have.'

'And of course we are still improving all the time too.'

'So what solution have you come up with?'

Freya explained next. 'We have developed a hydrogen based fuel cell that is self charging and never has to be replaced. Developing the cell was not difficult in itself but we have spent the last few months trying to reduce the size so that it is compact enough to use in even the smallest device, yet powerful enough to power the largest jet engines without having to use a billion of them, ha!'

'Yes, as Freya says, we have spent quite a while on this problem and have now got the cell down to the size of a pea….except it's flat and wafer thin. I'm sure, given more time we could get it even smaller, but the school board has decided it is imperative to get it out there now and work on further reductions in time.

We foresee the cells being in every device from lamps to televisions, computers, kitchen appliances, cars, bikes, trains and it only takes 5 to power a jet engine by the way.

There will be no need for electricity supplies to homes as each appliance will have its own and NO WIRES!!!!!!!!!!!!!!!

We are launching the pCell as it will be called, next week at a special news conference'

'And again, WOW. I can't wait to get mine. How much will they cost?'

'Absolutely nothing. They will be free to the world. Our gift, like the World Wide Web. Some things are much too important to be controlled by a few people and should be owned by us all.

Of course the appliances etc are not ready yet to use the pCells but we don't think that will take too long as only minor adjustments would need to be made to existing appliances, although of course new appliances will eventually be made using a lot less materials.

We thought about preparing manufacturers beforehand but this would have been far too difficult until we knew what working size we could get down to and also for security. We think anything smaller is likely to only be used in specialist equipment such as for medical use and the launch size will be a lasting product without many future changes required.

We have of course been concerned that the longer we took, the more chance someone will get there first and sell theirs for profit instead, so we have had to work as quickly and efficiently as we could as well as keeping it secret'

'But you feel happy that *I* won't spill the beans?'

'You're one of us, so we KNOW you won't'

They laughed and each felt a warm glow of understanding and belonging. They all knew they were going to be meeting up again in the very near future and looked forward with anticipation to achieving even more wondrous things together.

21 THE TOUR CONCLUDES

After the tour, they all met back as arranged and said their goodbyes to the girls so they could get back to getting ready for their exciting launch. Molly couldn't wait to meet up with them again and was also looking forward to the world's reaction to the next week's announcement, as were her parents.

They talked as they followed Beth along the path.

'I expect there will be an incredible demand for these fuel cells once the word is out. I know we could do with them at work. I bet there is not so much noise as there is now from the machinery'

'I expect the noise will still be there to some extent but perhaps reduced. Of course there will need to be some major modifications done to all sorts of equipment and this will take time and money. Perhaps even some brand new design will come out of all this.

There'll be a long term saving but the initial investment will need to be available so everything won't change totally overnight. Though we do have initial supplies of the pCells available in the billions and are still making them every day.'

'So you make them yourselves then? That does surprise me. Are they made here?'

'Yes Kim. Phoebe and her team have made their own manufacturing laboratory and storage system dedicated purely to the pCells where all the girls take it in turn to help out, but it is nothing like a normal factory.

They have built it on the far side of the estate and it is partially underground. Of course there is no danger of it, or any of the school grounds being seen from the air, though. Our very first intake of girls set up a holographic projection system all around the perimeter so that any aircraft going over will just see the original derelict estate.

The lab itself is a very clever design with a grass roof which overhangs the front glass walls at the front so it has lots of natural light inside. They have to keep it hygienically clean inside so no particles that shouldn't be there, get into the manufacturing process.

They have ample dedicated storage for while the pCells are waiting to be shipped out and they are proving extremely cheap to make. More so now that we have finished changing the whole estate over to the pCells and no longer have any fuel bills to pay!! We are actually still saving money when you take both into account so they cost us absolutely nothing to make and distribute as they easily pay their way.'

'It's all so incredible and about time too!! You are certainly making a difference here. Not only to the lives of these girls but everyday people all over the world'

'Don't forget, Kim, none of this would have been possible without Sarah.'

Kim felt a swell of pride and was now more looking forward to her inevitable chat with her Mum, than she had been a while ago.

'Now, as I said before, we won't go all the way over there today as it's so cold, but there are a couple more areas that I want to tell you about.' She indicated to her right.

'We have our own stables where all of the girls are expected to learn about riding and how to care for the horses. Similarly over in that direction we have our own engineering sheds where they all have to learn to repair and maintain all types of vehicles, from cars to lorries to motor bikes and we teach them to drive them also.'

'Not planes and trains then?' Mark smiled.

'Well.......actually yes. The trains are part of the compulsory engineering courses and we have our own airfield over in that direction and our own flight simulators. The girls learn to maintain and drive the trains and similarly maintain and fly all types of aircraft. We also have use of the flight simulators at NASA if we have anyone who wants to go into space flight'

'I should have known!' Mark was still smiling and couldn't help feeling a little envious.

'Over in that direction is our shooting range. The girls get full weapons training from guns to crossbows and they can practice with traditional long bows on our Archery range.

I think that's our main areas covered. Of course we have so much space here that if we need to set aside an area for something new, we are able to do so.

Ok. Shall we make our way back to the library and we can go over the domestics of life here at Trescotham Hall. I've just arranged for some more refreshments to be taken in there for us.'

Kim & Mark looked at each other and frowned quizzically. When on earth had she been able to arrange that.

22 DOMESTICS

Once they were settled again, back by the fire with mugs of steaming brew in front of them, and had finished with small talk, Beth continued with the domestics.

'Sleeping accommodation first. The girls all have their own rooms here with a large bed, build in cupboard and a work desk. All of the rooms are ensuite and the girls are expected to keep their rooms clean and tidy themselves.'

'Good luck with that!' Kim grimaced.

'We teach the girls how to look after themselves which includes not only self defence but also domestically. All of their clothes are provided for them so they don't have to bring anything with them except underwear. They must launder these themselves but we have a huge collection of clothes for all occasions which they can use as they wish and are laundered by our wonderful laundry team. However, the girls are not allowed to take this for granted so, once they are taught the correct way to launder clothes, they must each put in 8 hours a month working in the laundry.'

This time it was Molly's turn to pull a face.

'The same goes for the kitchens. All food is provided and placed in front of them when they need it but they are taught to make their own basic meals and have to help out both in the preparation and cleaning up for 8 hours a month also. We feel these things are just as important for the girls to learn and so that they don't take these chores, and the people who do them, for granted.'

'I definitely approve of THAT sentiment' said Kim

'Would I be able to bring my mobile phone?'

'You may not actually need it if your parents give us consent for you to be linked into our network using our Think Dots'

They all looked at each other again.

'What does that mean?'

'Let me explain. We have a unique method of communicating with each other and the outside world. Not surprisingly, it was our students that developed this system, some time ago now.

It involves each participant having a micro chip painlessly implanted just behind the ear, which they wear with an accompanying contact lens.'

'I don't like the sound of that first bit. It sounds like you'd be chipping my daughter just like you chip an animal so that you can track their movements'

'Don't worry, Mark. Of course it can be used to find someone in an emergency but Molly would have complete control over the device and could turn it on and off as she wishes. Please be assured, this is by no means compulsory so if you and Kim feel uncomfortable about it in any way, Molly does not have to be implanted.'

'*Yes, Molly does*' thought Molly.

'We do find though that all of the students find it more useful to be in the network, eventually. Let me explain a little more about the Think Dots and you can talk it over when you get home.

As I said, the chip is implanted painlessly under the skin behind the ear. It is so minute that it is undetectable and won't be picked up by airport scanners or cause any interference with any other electrical item.

Similarly the contact lens element is perfectly safe around other equipment and even works underwater. It's just like a computer screen and relays any information that the wearer wants to put up there. Several screens can be put up together if they need to compare data, for example, or if they wish to video conference with several people at once.

They can project the screen if they prefer, so that it appears to float in mid air. This is in case they want to discuss it with others, for example. They can do anything really that you could do on your computer or any smart phone and even more.

It is controlled by thought. There is a knack to it that Molly should learn easily. In a way it is just a further enhancement to her almost telepathic abilities. It works to communicate between the girls and the staff, but it also works to be able to make a normal voice call either my speaking out loud or by thinking the words, so she could use it to call home, for example.'

'Doesn't sound as bad as I first thought then'

'Of course we can track everyone on the network just like you can track someone using a mobile phone so it has it's uses if we need to get hold of someone or they are in danger, but the users can block this if they so wish, to protect their privacy, at any time. They just have to think the correct command.'

Beth paused to sip her tea and let what she had said sink in.

'Well, I think I'm in Sci Fi heaven!!!!!! Can I get a set of these so I can ring Kim at home without the boss knowing and then sit back and play video games while I'm pretending to work?'

Kim frowned at him.

'Sorry, Mark, these can only be used by people with Ants at the moment. They seem more easily able to use the thought control. We are working on making some for Norms but they won't be ready just yet. We are hoping to be able to get them to market over the next few years and as cheaply as possible to keep the retail price down.'

'That's a shame. I can't wait to try them out so if you need a guinea pig......'

'Ha! You'll be the first we call, Mark, don't worry.'

Beth continued.

'Well as I said we are very flexible with school hours and holidays but for safety reasons we do have some school rules in place such as getting permission to leave the school grounds but I have put together a simple pack for you to take with you. For obvious reasons only the school name is on these documents'

'I understand now why you don't have a website and why everything has to be kept top secret but I have to admit, I was a bit freaked out when I first got your letter'

'I'm sorry we unsettled you Kim, but I'm sure, if you agree to send Molly to the school, you would want the same security in place to protect her'

'Yes of course. Thank you Beth'

'I think there is only one last thing to talk about, unless you have any questions about anything so far'

'I was just wondering about the staff. Do they sleep here as well?'

'Yes, mostly. I have my own bungalow in the grounds where my husband and I and my stepdaughter live. She is also a pupil at the school. My deputy, Lauren Franklyn, also has her own bungalow. One of us is on the school grounds at all times in case of emergencies. We have a range of staff accommodation from rooms for single teachers which are similar to the girl's rooms and also we have family suites available for those with families.

Some of the teachers and most of the other staff chose to live away from the school but close by, some in the nearby village. We also have a very discreet security team living on site who monitor visitors and look for anything unusual.'

'Very discreet! I didn't notice anybody, did you Kim?'

'No, not at all'

'That's the idea! Now, is there anything else you want to ask me?'

'We're bound to think of something we forgot to ask, on the way home'

'That won't be a problem. I have allocated the phone number you originally called me on as a private line for just you and Mark to use, so either of you can get straight through to me at any time.' By now they were not surprised by this technology and indeed it was now one of the less impressive examples they had seen that day.

'OK. The last thing we need to discuss is finances'

'We can't afford to pay fees of any sort. I thought the school was free or is this where you tell us the catch'

'No, I think you have misunderstood Mark. All of Molly's educational and personal needs will be met and paid for by the school and she will also receive a small monthly allowance for all her other needs. However, we expect that in quite a short time, despite Molly's education and development being the top priority, her endeavours will start to earn money for the school and also for herself.

The most important developments we make, we of course give free to the world but we also gain advantage from them, for example by using the pCells to eliminate our energy costs. Other developments, such as the diet pills and the Think Dots, although we will sell them as cheaply as possible, will make us a very considerable profit. We will share that profit with all of the girls, with the most to the girl who developed it along with her team.

So when I said we need to discuss finances, I meant we need to discuss things like getting Molly a bank account to have any such funds paid into. I suggest an account initially with one of you as joint holder, so that you can have an element of control over her spending until she gets used to handling her own money. We naturally have our own financial advisers that can help and advise her along the way. Molly will be an extremely wealthy woman one day'

Kim and Mark were lost for words. As if their emotions hadn't been on enough of a rollercoaster already today!

23 IN THE HOT TUB

Kim laid back in the hot tub and finally started to relax as the bubbles manipulated her tensed up muscles.

'What an incredible way to end an incredible day! Can you believe everything we've seen and heard today, love?'

'I'm sure I'll wake up in a mo, but this water is definitely sending me to sleep so I must be awake.....if you know what I mean'

'Err....just about. Do you think Beth is listening to us now?'

'I hope not but she seems to have very high moral standards for herself and the school so I doubt she would eavesdrop unless it was crucial. Where did our Molly go?'

'She went to say good bye to those girls she met. She thinks we've already decided to send her here even before we have discussed it properly'

'I know, Kim, but we have already decided, haven't we? How could we possible refuse her such an opportunity as this?'

'True, but it won't be easy for us back home without her. Even the boys will miss her like crazy even though they sometimes fall out. What on earth are we going to say to them about all this. We need to work out how much we can tell them and how much to keep to ourselves in case they blab to anyone'

'Perhaps your Mam could help in that respect'

'Good grief! I'd almost forgotten I've THAT conversation to come.'

'Well, don't be too hard on her. I think it's fantastic what she's achieved here. It's made me look at her in quite a different light now'

'Yes, I suppose I'm beginning to understand her myself a bit better now. I've just thought! Dad's got to know of course but I wonder if the little two do! They'd better not have been told before me or there'll be trouble. And if they don't know, I bet I won't be able to say anything to them. How frustrating!!'

The family had always referred to Kim's much younger sisters Laura & Betsy as 'the little two' despite them now being aged twenty five and twenty six!

'Look, stop getting yourself in a tis till you've spoken to her. I doubt if your sisters know. Laura doesn't have any kids and Betsy has a son so there would be no need for either of them to be told and it certainly looks like this place is strictly on a need-to-know basis. And besides, you're supposed to be relaxing in this tub, so make the most of it while you can'

'You're right, as usual. Let's not talk any more until we get out of here'

Silence for a few minutes.

'Our   Molly   is   gonna   be   rich………….
Yeahhhhhhhhhhhhhh'

They both collapsed into fits of laughter.

24 MOTHER AND DAUGHTER HEART TO HEART

'Hi Mam!'

'Hi sweetheart! I've put the kettle on' They kissed.

'Thanks for having the boys yesterday. Did they behave?'

'I didn't see much of them all day. They were next door with Ethan playing on his new game. They only came in when they were falling out over who's turn it was next. I think Betsy had kicked them off the game and told them to play with something else if they couldn't play nicely. They were as good as gold over here. They're always good for me. It's you they like to wind up!'

'True but you do spoil them with sweets and chocolate'

'That's what Nans are for! Tea or coffee love?'

'Tea please Mam'

'Shall we sit in the room or at the kitchen table?'

'I think here at the kitchen table is where we always do our serious talking' she sat down. 'Where's Dad?'

'He's over at Laura's just finishing off the repairs to her guttering. That heavy snow had pulled it all down so he's fitted new brackets now it's all thawed, before we get another snowfall. I don't like him climbing up those ladders. I've told Laura to make sure she holds them at the bottom when he goes up. He's not as young as he used to be.'

'He's not *that* old either Mam and he's quite physically fit for an old codger'

'I know but I don't know what we'd all do without him' Neither of them wanted to entertain those thoughts so they quickly moved on.

'So you had an interesting day yesterday?'

Kim suddenly burst into floods of tears.

'What am I crying for, stupid woman. Sorry Mam, I don't know where this lot has come from' between sobs 'I'm not unhappy'

'I know, don't worry sweetheart' she held her daughter. 'It's perfectly natural. It's like when you have something on your mind and you are holding all these emotions in check quite easily without realising it and then somebody asks you how you are and it all comes out like a dam has burst.'

'That's it exactly' she starts to dry her tears. 'It was such a shock to find out you had kept this whole other life from me…… from us. Does Dad know and the little two?'

'Dad does of course. He's been with me all the way but I haven't told your sisters either.'

'I can't help feeling a bit betrayed Mam. Surely you could have told me at some stage.'

'I intended to at first, when I thought I was just setting up an excellent, if quite normal school. I didn't want to tell any of you until it was ready to open. Don't forget, I had never done anything like this before; I wasn't entirely sure I could do it, so I didn't want the embarrassment of failing to get it up and running, broadcast to my family. Dad agreed.

Remember, this was when Molly was a toddler and Harry a few months old and you had just fallen pregnant with Lucas so you had enough to think about. The little two were obnoxious teenagers causing us double trouble at every turn. They wouldn't have cared less anyway as they were at that 'self absorbed, angry about everything and out of sync with the rest of the world' stage. We'd thought of waiting till they clicked back in sync and became normal human beings again but that takes years.' They smiled at each other and both felt a bit lighter.

'Then of course, before I could tell you, we found out about the girls with Ants' Kim couldn't help chuckling to herself hearing her mother use the girls description of their enhanced abilities.

'Of course when you get a personal request from your Prime Minister, what's a girl to do?' This time they both collapsed in fits of laughter.

'But seriously, from that day my highest priority has been the safety and security of the girls. Tell me, what would you've done differently if you were in my shoes?'

Kim thought for a minute.

'No…..I would have done exactly the same. But surely since then, particularly when you became aware that Molly may have Ants.'

'I wanted Molly to have as normal a childhood as possible. You're not telling me you don't look at her differently now.'

'I still love her bones so don't think I don't!'

'I don't mean that. Now you know how intelligent she is and how capable, you'll quite rightly, at this stage, start treating her like someone much older. I wanted her to have her childhood for as long as possible. I know it has been difficult for her to keep everything bottled in but that's all part of growing up for most young people anyway and she is better able to cope than most'

'When did you first notice Molly's Ants? I suppose I've always had an awareness without really thinking about it.'

'From birth, I knew from her reactions that her hearing was excellent and she focused her eyes from day one and looked right at you. Of course I didn't know about the other girls then and even when I did, I didn't think Molly was really enhanced as the others had only gained their abilities at puberty.

So I kept an eye on her anyway but it soon became clear how intelligent she was. We know she was speaking clearly straight away and skipped baby talk altogether. I had a feeling when I sat and read to her that she could read the books as well as I could.

Once I got to know more about the girls and their Ants, it became clear that Molly had them too, but she was unique so far, as it seemed she had been born with these extraordinary skills. When I employed Beth Drake to run the school, I confided in her about Molly and she agreed with me that it would be best just to observe her for the time being and only step in if she needed us to, until the time was right to offer her a place at the school.'

'I suppose you had to get advice from someone and Beth would have been my choice in your position'

'Of course, I'm proud to say, my granddaughter has handled herself admirably! I know she has taught herself to control some of her Ants and she has learnt to hide them so that she fits in at school.

I'm proud of the boys as well! I know they are aware that Molly has special abilities but they almost subconsciously know it would be bad to tell anyone.'

'Yes, I suppose we all just thought of Molly as being a bit different without *really* thinking about why. You know, it's just Molly!'

'I suppose it's time I told the little two as well'

'Oh yes please! You know what Laura's like! She has no children of her own but she'd give me no end of grief about sending Molly to a boarding school at her age. She still might, even when you tell her!'

'Don't worry. I'll be seeing them both tomorrow anyway so I'll tell them then and I'll make it clear to Laura to butt out!'

'Thanks Mam. I hope you know how proud I am of you, despite all the other feelings I had at first. I think they were just shock'

'Thank you darling. I'm proud of you too.'

'Oh hi Dad. You managed not to fall off your ladder then.'

25 MOLLY SETTLES IN

Molly loved her new room. It was bright and sunny and extremely spacious. She still couldn't believe she had it all to herself! She was just down the hall from Phoebe and Freya and she had a lovely view of the grounds which she would enjoy more in the summer when she could sit out on her own patio just outside the French doors.

She'd been at Trescotham Hall almost two weeks now and her room was already looking and feeling like home. She had family photos next to her bed and her iPod dock too. Strictly speaking she didn't need that as she could play music online through her Think Dots but sometimes she liked to have it on quietly in the background while she read or worked on her Think Dot. Sometimes she liked to fall asleep to it too.

Her luxurious ceiling to floor curtains were extremely pretty in an abstract pattern of pinks and purples. The plump pillows and thick duvet were also covered with the same material to match. It was the first time she had had her own bathroom with her own shower and she had taken time to set out some of her bath crystals and soaps so that they looked really pretty and she put the rest away in the cupboard out of sight.

She didn't miss Mum, Dad and the boys as much as she had thought she would. That was because she saw them every evening on the Think Dot while they were having a good chat. Her parents were finally making use of the webcam that had been sitting in the box since Christmas.

'Hi Sis! How's it going at Super Hero school? Have you discovered any new Superpowers yet?'

'I've TOLD you, Harry, it's NOT Super Hero school and STOP calling my abilities Superpowers!!!!! Everyone will have them eventually. We just got them a bit sooner, that's all! Now stop acting like an annoying little brother and put Mam and Dad on for me. Where's Lucas?'

'He's at his friend's house. What's up? Your Superpowers didn't tell you that?'

'Grrrrrrrrrrrr, brothers!!!!!!'

Molly had also called her Nan & Granddad twice a week as usual. She hadn't been home yet but she intended to go this next weekend for Lucas' birthday party. She was looking forward to the hugs and kisses she knew would be showered upon her.

Molly had also had a long chat with her Nan before she left for the school. They had always been very close but it was good to finally talk openly to her about her Ants. She really appreciated (and on some level, knew) that her Nan had been looking out for her for all these years.

She had been invited to the launch of the pCell. Naturally it hadn't been held at the school for security reasons and had been held at Lady Catherine's estate. Lady Catherine had addressed the press and had implied that it was one of her own companies that had invented the pCell, which of course it was.

She didn't mention the age of the inventors or anything about the girls or the school and with her confidence and experience so evident, the reporters accepted her version of events. She told them that one of her companies had invented a power source that would revolutionise our use of energy and would put a stop to our huge affect on the Earth's climate and the resultant danger to life.

When she explained about the pCells and said they would be free to all, there was a huge cheer around the room that was deafening. Of course there were some sceptics but Lady Catherine's assurances seemed to placate them for a while. She told them that more information would be provided over the coming weeks and that the next stage was to start contacting manufacturers about adapting appliances and vehicles etc to accommodate the new energy source.

In fact, Molly was told, several of the ex pupils of the school had been employed to act as technical advisers to the companies and also at further press conferences if required. They had spent time with Phoebe and Freya at the production site and were well versed in all aspects of the pCell. This was to protect the younger girls and not raise suspicions about the school.

As predicted, the announcement caused a huge reaction around the world! Most of it was extremely positive but of course the oil and gas companies were far from happy. Their businesses collapsed overnight. Phoebe assured her it was their own fault for not investing in clean renewable energy when they had the chance.

Molly knew Phoebe still had sympathy for the ordinary workers that would now have to look for alternative work. She said she hoped some of them could be employed to help with the huge change over that now had to be done.

26 MOLLY'S FIRST PROJECT

Molly was getting more used to the rules of the school now. Not that there were that many. Of course security was the main concern. Molly knew who she could discuss the school with and who she couldn't. She expected not to be able to just leave the school grounds without getting permission.

What did surprise her though was the level of trust that she and all the girls were given. Individual privacy was also very important to the school, as she had been told by Ms Drake at her induction. Their Ants meant it was possible for all of the girls to eavesdrop on each other and the teaching staff or to spy on each other and this was not acceptable.

They had to control themselves so that they only listened to conversations or observed people in the room they were in and everyone understood this to be the case. Therefore if you wanted a private conversation with someone and there were others in the room, you had to take them out to another room. No one was allowed to spy in any other room. Even when they were in the classrooms or outdoors learning to enhance their abilities further, they were trusted not to spy or eavesdrop on the rest of the school.

This seemed to work extremely well over the years with a very few exceptions, she had been told. This intrigued Molly but Ms Drake somehow made it difficult for her to read anything from her. However, embarrassingly, Ms Drake had managed to read Molly quite well. She went on to tell her that she would learn to control her Ants to such an extent, that she could mask them for a short time at will to prevent others with Ants from taking advantage. Molly had blushed at this.

She already had full control over her enhanced sight and hearing but she had already managed to improve and better control some of her other Ants, like reading thoughts and emotions and stopping others reading her and she had had chance to fully try others that she'd had to keep more hidden, like her fast running speed and her ability with languages. Her favourite so far though had been when she had tried out the new Ant that she hadn't been aware of.

She had been swimming before of course but had not tried to swim underwater for any length of time. She was a bit nervous at first but after only a few tries, she found it becoming more and more like second nature to her. She was soon swimming around and around the pool under the water. She was then given a time trial by Ms Juniper, the teacher in charge at the Aqua Centre and she caused a sensation as she didn't seem to have a time limit on how long she could stay under, unlike the other girls. She was able to stay under much longer than anyone before and they gave up after an hour as it looked like she was quite as at home in the water as she was in the air!

She had started her survival training, which she was not as keen on as she thought she would be: she hoped she would enjoy it more as she progressed and she understood how necessary this sort of training was for all the girls. They had to be prepared in case any other country decided to use their Ants against them or even if an individual or group of individuals went rogue. And of course, the Prime Minister at the time had made a special request to *her* Nan that the girls be so prepared!

That morning she had had her first stint in the laundry, which she had been dreading but she had actually really enjoyed. She had never laughed so much in all her life! The laundry team were certainly a bunch of characters who told jokes and made wise cracks all the time as well as getting through mountains of laundry. She was actually looking forward to working there again. She hoped she would have as much fun in the kitchens the next day.

That afternoon she had had another meeting with Ms Drake to see how she was settling in and to plan any other activities that she felt she wanted to include in her education. Ms Drake had gone through her progress so far and was very pleased with her.

She had asked Molly if there was any particular subject or project that she wanted to take on. Molly had been thinking about this for a while. She had been inspired by Phoebe and Freya and wanted to take on a project that would have the same far reaching benefits. She wanted to work on a new mode of personal transport that could be used alone or by the whole family together.

'A car, you mean' joked Ms Drake.

'No, not a conventional car, but now we have the pCells, I think a radical new design could be produced.'

'Tell me what you have in mind'

'I envisage individual pods so that one person could travel alone, to work for example but they could easily fasten together and open into one larger unit so that the whole family could travel together if they wish'

'That sounds very interesting, Go on'

'I don't want them to travel along the road though as I see them being able to go much further and faster to the extent that families could use them to travel on holiday instead of going by commercial airlines' She waited nervously for Ms Drake's reaction.

'Ok…..So how would they travel?'

'I see them being airborne but not high in the sky like a jet. Just perhaps above the houses would be the main cruising height. They wouldn't need to use roads except when they land and maybe as an option for very short journeys. Initially, unless we develop something similar for commercial use, I think that would leave the roads much clearer for lorries etc.

They would have no obstacles like water or hills as they could fly higher if they needed to and I hope that one day each individual would have their own that could join with lots of others if many people want to travel together. They would be programmable so that a driver would not be required and of course they would be ultra safe as I would build in all the necessary safety features such as anti-collision devices.'

'You certainly have given this a lot of thought Molly. Are you serious about wanting to take this further?'

'Yes, I think I am. At least I want to try and see what I can come up with.'

'Excellent! I want you to draw up a plan of action for me so that I know what facilities you will need and I'll then arrange as much help with the project as you need. I know some of the girls are finishing up on their own projects and I am sure they would be more than happy to help you with yours'

So, now she was back in her room wondering where on earth to start!

27 FAVOURITE TEACHER

She'd agonised half the night about what to put on her plan of action. Of course it was great not to have to hide her super intelligence but she was still a child after all and still lacked experience in most aspects of life. She knew Ms Drake would offer help either herself or from one of the other girls but Molly didn't want to have to ask on her very first project. Not till she had to.

She knew there was no rush. She had her survival training to complete with her endurance test at the end and she knew this was not optional, but she didn't intend to go all out to break any records. She was hoping to delay her hot and cold weather training if she could, until after she had completed her project, as she didn't know how she could fit in several trips abroad with everything else she had to do.

She decided the first place to start on her project was with some sort of basic design. She was quite good at drawing but she found some design software available in the 'Cloud', the internet based way of sharing resources. She was wondering how secure a method this would be, when she received a call from her friend Phoebe.

'You're up late'

'You too. I wasn't sure if you would be switched off for the night but I thought I'd try. What's keeping you up? You're not finding it too much already are you?' Both girls laughed.

'No, I have to give my first action plan to Ms Drake and my mind's all a whirl at the minute'

'Well, I'm here if you need some help, don't forget. With anything.'

'Oh, actually, there is something. I've just been looking at some design software in the Cloud. Would this be safe to use? I don't want anyone to be able to get hold of any of my designs.'

'There's no problem using anything in the Cloud. We have the best computer security there is, all designed by our own alumni of course. Once information or software has been accessed by anyone at the school, an extremely strong firewall is automatically built around it and several false IP addresses are emitted so no one can track back to us this way'

'Excellent, thanks Phoebe. By the way, did you want something when you called me?'

'Yes, I was wondering if you would be interested in helping me organise a surprise birthday party for Ms Franklyn? It's her birthday week after next.'

Ms Franklyn was one of the girls favourite teachers. She had the same beautiful big brown eyes that Ms Drake had but she was taller and had dark nut brown shoulder length hair. Ms Franklyn and Ms Drake were often taken for sisters.

Rumour had it that Trescotham Hall was the only place that Lauren Franklyn had ever been truly happy. So much so that she couldn't bear to leave the school when her studies were complete so she stayed on as a teacher.

She had not had a very happy childhood. Both of her parents had died when she was a baby and she had been from foster home to foster home as she had been a particularly difficult child to get through to. Initially it was because she was excruciatingly shy but then she just refused to speak or interact with any grown ups unless it was absolutely necessary and she didn't think it was on most occasions.

She struggled at school to such an extent that the teachers thought she had severe learning difficulties except that every now and then, when she felt like it, she would show them she was in fact very bright.

Then her Ants arrived and totally changed her life. Of course, all the girls felt this way but for Lauren it was a much bigger change. At first she wasn't sure herself if she was going crazy or not. Then she started to experiment and realised a small fraction of what she could do. It was one particular experiment that was to change her life forever when it brought her to the attention of Sarah Thompson and Beth Drake.

Lauren had a feeling she could run extremely fast so she wanted to put it to the test after school one day. It was getting dark, which was better in case she was seen, so she went down to the local running track at King Edward Stadium.

Her hearing and vision Ants still made her wince sometimes as she felt blasted with sound and vision but she managed to use them to make sure there was no one about. She started at a normal pace to warm her muscles and gradually ran faster and faster until she reached an incredible speed and just cruised along for a while. She had never felt more alive.

She gradually slowed her speed until she was just jogging along and continued out of the stadium and headed back towards her foster home. She was just jogging past the park when her acute hearing heard a terrified scream being stifled. She picked up the pace and headed into the park towards the sound.

She didn't think twice when she saw the youth in a baseball cap straddled across the thrashing young woman with his hands around her throat. She just lunged herself at speed towards him and sent him careering away and trying to save himself from plunging into the nearby lake.

Lauren grabbed the woman and hauled her to her feet, with a strength that surprised both her and the already traumatised woman.

'Quick, we need to get you out of here'

'But who saved me. Was it your Dad? Where did he go?'

'No there's only me, now let's get moving'

The woman was more than a little confused but was still in shock and her legs were only just holding her up. This little girl started to guide her towards the path and streetlamps towards the safety of the open park gates where she could already see lots of people passing by.

All of a sudden Lauren felt a sharp pain in her side, then another, then another. She heard the piercing scream of the woman and turned to see her attacker holding a long sharp knife that was dripping with blood, which Lauren knew was her own. She threw the hardest punch she could at her attacker's jaw before she collapsed in a heap and let the dark comfort of unconsciousness cradle her to sleep.

28 HOME AT LAST

When Lauren came round, she was already starting to heal. There was a crowd of people around her and their attacker was still unconscious next to her. The woman was being comforted by an elderly couple who had wrapped the man's coat around her and the ambulance and police sirens were signalling their imminent arrival.

Lauren thought it was time she got out of there but she still felt very weak and couldn't see how she was going to make her escape unnoticed. She got to her feet amidst calls for her to sit down, don't move young lady, and take it easy there girl.

The police headed straight for their attacker. They had been on his trail for a while now but had never managed to catch up with him. He had a broken jaw and looked like he was going to be out for the count for a while yet.

The woman was being attended to while she gave the police her fantastic story about her eleven year old rescuer and another medic was trying unsuccessfully to examine Lauren's wounds.

'I'm fine, I told you. He just scratched me. I have a thick jacket on and thick skin' she said through gritted teeth.

'There's a lot of blood about and you're the only one that's been bleeding so you may be hurt and don't realise it'

'Please........leave me alone. I've told you I'm fine and I have to get home now or I'll be in deep trouble. See how that lady is, quick I think they need your help over there'

The young woman had started to be sick all over the other medic so thankfully it caused a diversion and she managed to get up and slip deeper into the crowd, then onto the edge of the crowd and finally into the shadows and away. She was gaining strength with each hurried step until she was able to jog the remaining way home.

But how was she going to explain the holes in her jacket and top? She threw her jacket in a skip as she passed. She could say she just lost it somewhere. She could probably wash and sew her top herself and she didn't think her foster parents would notice all the blood if she was careful, as she usually went straight up to her room when she got home anyway.

The next day it was in the papers about a mystery child who had rescued a young woman, incapacitated her attacker and had miraculously recovered from a horrific knife attack and had run away. To Sarah Thompson and Beth Drake, it had 'Ants' written all over it.

Through Lady Catherine's contacts they managed to arrange for the local authority to grant them an interview with her whilst her social worker sat outside the room. Lauren was particularly quiet that day and really not in the mood to meet with strangers. 'Have I been identified from last night or am I being sent to yet another foster home', she thought.

But there was something different about the two women who greeted her, particularly one of them. Lauren sensed something about the one called Ms Drake but she couldn't quite get a hold of what it was. Then something incredible happened. It was as if this woman had 'let her in' and she knew without doubt that she was just like her!

Lauren was stunned and totally forgot her promise to herself to keep absolutely quiet and say nothing, as she had done most of her life around all adults. She could hardly believe what they were telling her about other girls like her and a school where she could live and learn how to improve her abilities and learn new skills. She wanted to be cautious and to imagine it not being a very nice place at all, but she was getting so many positive, happy ......images almost, from Ms Drake that she almost dared hope that her life was finally about to change for the good.

They told her she could be admitted to the school very quickly due to her circumstances and that her current foster parents and even the local authority, didn't need to be told anything except that she had been accepted at a new boarding school that would look after all of her needs. Sarah knew that, if necessary, her links to the Prime Minister would cut through any red tape that may be thrown at her. She felt it was vital to get this vulnerable young girl to the school as soon as possible, hopefully the next day.

For the first time in Lauren's life, she had a feeling of absolute exhilaration and anticipation for her future. She knew she was going to have a very unusual and fulfilling life from now on and couldn't help thinking that at last, she was finally going home.

29 CHATTING

'Yes of course I'd love to help. It's a good job it isn't this weekend though. I'm going home for my brother's birthday.'

'Great then. I'll catch up with you tomorrow and we can go over a few ideas. There's a couple more girls want to get involved too so it should be fun. Now, we need to keep it from her so how are you doing at blocking? We don't want you to accidentally give everything away when you're in the same room as her'

'No need to worry, I'm doing really well. I put a permanent block up all the time now'

'Really!! Wow, that's better than me. I can only last a few hours if I really concentrate. The rumours about you are true then.'

'Rumours? What rumours?'

Phoebe laughed.

'That already you're one of the best and brightest students that we've ever had here, of course'

'Well I have had my Ants since I was born so I suppose I've had much longer to practice…..and get it wrong'

They both laughed and said their goodbyes.

Molly laid back on her pillow and reluctantly began thinking about her project again. It was late and she was tired so she finally gave the close command to shut down the screen floating in front of her eyes and got snuggled in for a peaceful nights sleep.

30 PROGRESS SO FAR

Over the next six months Molly really felt that she was improving every single day and she was very happy and contented with her life. She even enjoyed the survival training now. She couldn't get out of the hot and cold field trips as she had hoped and had been abroad several times already.

She'd loved the heat in the Sahara and learnt how to find water and food and what to use to build a shelter against the sun and the freezing cold nights. She didn't mind the cold and thin air up in the Himalayas either, and loved the wildlife in the Arctic, perhaps most of all. They all had such easy going thoughts and happy natures.

She felt her Ants were almost the best they could be. Her speed and agility was the best in the school and she was exceptionally good at hand to hand combat using her newly acquired Martial Arts skills. It was a pity she couldn't try them out on her brothers but she had also had to learn the discipline that comes along with such ancient skills.

One of her favourite Ants was her language skills. She had been to spend time with families in Turkey, Egypt, Venezuela and Japan and loved conversing with them in their native tongue and learning all about their different cultures. She had made some good friends along the way, who regularly called her for a chat and to reminisce and offer invitations for a revisit.

She was still working hard to develop her full potential with controlling electronics and felt she still had some way to go with this one. It was so unique that both her, and her favourite teacher Ms Franklyn were learning together.

Sometimes Molly found that she almost got lost in the circuitry. She would put her hand above an object and feel the heat. Using her mind she could make her way quite easily to the start controls and get the gadget fired up. She would feel her way around and manage to work all of the controls this way with no problems.

However, a couple of times, she had had great difficulty getting out again and this had frightened her a bit….and Ms Franklyn, so they were taking things slowly until they could fathom out what the problem was and perhaps learn a bit more about how this particular Ant worked.

By now she could have easily gained Doctorates in all the basic academic subjects. It helped to have perfect recall of course! So she no longer had to do those basic subjects. The students were constantly monitored and their progress measured so they did not actually have to sit exams. Anyway, it would have been totally unfair and a huge risk to their privacy to sit the same exams as the Norms.

Some of the employer's the girls were eventually placed with had invested in the school or knew the girls were exceptional without actually knowing the full story about their Ants, so they were not looking for paper qualifications. If Sarah Thompson or Lady Catherine Sampson recommended someone, you didn't need to ask questions because you knew they were going to be top notch.

She had managed to get home several times for short breaks. She had been a bit concerned that she might have been bored and itching to get back to Trescotham, particularly now that her mind seemed to crave more and more knowledge, but she had her Think Dot, so after very enjoyable days out and time spent with the family, she satisfied that particular itch by laying back on her bed and studying.

Molly was a natural at computer sciences and loved to help out on projects with the girls who specialised in that area, although it was not what Molly wanted to do as a career. She was purely honing her computer skills to help with everything else she did, particularly her own project.

She still loved her time spent with the comedians in the laundry but a bit less so in the kitchens. It was always too manic in there at meal times, but they were still good people and she was becoming quite good at serving meals and clearing away after so many at once.

A few months before, she had been intrigued when she had been asked to break a special code. She had no idea who for, or what it was all about but her grandmother had asked her, which she had thought at the time was a bit odd. She'd told her that a couple of the other girls had tried but couldn't quite crack the final piece. She had been expressly asked NOT to try to find out any more, but just to try to find the answer, as it was extremely important.

Molly had taken only two days to find the solution. There had been a flaw in the work done already that was putting the others off the trail. Molly had started from the beginning and, once she had discovered the error, she had found the rest very simple.

This was to be the first of many such mysterious requests which all seemed to come directly from her grandmother, with instructions not to delve any deeper than what was being asked of her.

Several times since she had been here, she was asked to go over to the local hospital to help with a particularly difficult case. She had gone pretending to be a visitor and had used her unique Ant to see and smell where the problem was. She had then discussed what she had found with one of the doctors, in private. Of course this doctor was an ex pupil of the school so no suspicions were aroused. She thought she got most satisfaction from this Ant as she could actually see that she was directly helping someone who needed her.

Molly was still close with Phoebe, although she knew Freya was not at all happy about this. Freya had not wanted to be involved with helping to plan Ms Franklyn's very successful birthday bash, once she knew Phoebe had asked Molly to help. They might all have had super intelligence but they were still young girls after all!

Molly was too busy to bother too much about Freya's petty jealousies. She was still doing her best to get close to her however, as she felt this was the best way to help diffuse the situation a little and she felt Freya was thawing a bit towards her. But Molly had a new BFF now, called Daisy.

31 FRIENDS GET TOGETHER

Daisy had come to the school a few weeks after Molly had and the girls really hit it off right from the beginning. She was a cute girl with mousy brown hair to just below her jaw line, deep blue eyes and a smattering of freckles across her nose. She looked much younger than she was. Her room was just across the hall from Molly's so she had helped her settle in.

Daisy had two younger brothers too but also an older sister who hadn't developed Ants. This had made things very difficult for her at home and her parents had not been any help at all. They didn't seem to be interested in their children much and only thought of them as an annoyance that interfered in their busy lives.

They were well cared for physically but Daisy could never remember the hugs and kisses that she had seen from Molly's family, the first time she had gone home with her for the weekend. Nor could Daisy ever remember either of her parents showing the slightest interest in what she had been doing or what she had to say. Molly was the first person who had actually given her much attention at all and she felt closer to her in a few days than she had to her own sister all of her life.

Daisy had been struggling to control her sight and hearing Ants when she first arrived and they had often blasted her head nearly right off and left her with a splitting headache. Molly had quickly helped her learn to control them so now she could function better day to day and concentrate on improving her other abilities.

Molly had eventually come up with an action plan for her Travel Pods project and had submitted it to Ms Drake. After very careful study and a few revisions to the plan, Ms Drake had eventually given her the go ahead to proceed, but not until all her basic training had been completed and her academic subjects had been learnt to at least degree level.

She had now satisfied those provisos and she expected to have a bit more free time now so she was ready to get her team together.

Daisy and Phoebe had already agreed to join her and Freya was still thinking about it but Molly hoped she would say yes. Freya had much needed experience after working on Phoebe's project but she said she was in the preliminary stages of a project of her own, so Molly understood why she was hesitant but felt there was something else going on with her too.

The three girls met up in one of the student lounges initially just to chat about the prototype. They had been allocated their own high tech workshop and would be spending most of their time there over the next few months.

Molly had already pre warned her family that she would have to break her routine of going home every other weekend but they were more than happy and very excited that she was already working on a project of her own.

'Ok, it looks like it will be just us three for now. Freya may join us later but if we really need additional help I'm sure we can find someone. Before I send a copy of the plans of the prototype to your Think Dots, I want you to look at a demonstration video that I've mocked up.' She paused while she thought the correct commands to send the video to their Think Dots. 'OK, sit back and enjoy and we'll talk at the end'

The girls relaxed in their chairs and started watching the demo.

32 INTRODUCING THE TRAVEL POD

The video showed a pretty little avenue with several houses with Travel Pods standing on the driveways. The camera panned down to one particular drive where a man welcomed the viewers and started to explain all about the single person vehicle.

It certainly didn't look like anything else on the roads, or in the air for that matter. It was rectangular and looked very sleek with rounded corners and had a solid bottom half and a see through dome on top. It had two 'legs', one at the front in the centre and one at the back in the centre. Attached to each leg, going vertically across the pod there was a ski-like runner with four small wheels fitted inside.

The presenter was just explaining that the legs retracted on take off and folded away invisibly underneath and the bottom part of the pod was used for storage and could hold two large suitcases. There were also special hidden magnets all the way round that only attracted other pods when they were both activated, so that pods could be attached to travel together.

The man pressed his palm to the door and it gracefully slid across revealing the interior. At the same time, the seat inside turned to face him and lowered to allow the man to sit. He explained that each pod was programmed to the individuals biometrics - handprint, retina and voice and you could use voice commands, rather than touch if you preferred. He also said that the chair could be lowered or raised to the easiest height for the individual using it.

The seat looked extremely comfortable and had arm rests with a drinks holder and a hidden food tray. It had a high head rest with small speakers on either side. The speakers had directional sound so they could be set so that only the listener could hear them and no one else, so headphones were not required, or the sound wave could be widened for when pods were travelling together.

The man was now demonstrating how the seat folded flat into a bed for long journeys. The headrest inflated into a pillow and as it slowly reclined a shelf was revealed with a blanket neatly folded upon it. He explained that no seat belts were necessary as, in the extremely unlikely event of an accident or malfunction, an inflatable safety net would cover the whole pod and gently return the occupant to earth or would float if they were above water.

Having put the seat back upright, he showed how it could swivel round 360 degrees and be positioned in any direction. He explained that the pods came in individual sizes to fit the occupant and there were special sizes for children and small babies that could only be controlled by the attached adult pod.

Accessory pods would also be available for those that required them and would be particularly useful for those planning long journeys or going on holiday. There would be an extra luggage pod, a kitchen pod, a loo pod, a dressing pod, a shower pod and also a pet pod. By attaching the right combination it would be the equivalent of taking your home on holiday with you.

He then turned to the control panel. He explained that the pod could be programmed just like a Sat Nav with the post code, address or place of interest and the pod would take the shortest route to get you there. You didn't have to drive it as it was all automated. You could also just set it for a scenic drive with no destination if you wanted to. When families or friends travel together, one pod is designated as master controller once they were all linked up.

It was perfectly safe, he explained as the pod was fitted with anti-collision sensors and could not break the speed or height limits that each country would impose. There was also expected to be an internationally agreed speed limit over large bodies of water such as the oceans.

The pod had the added advantage of being self cleaning too. He then opened a small door under the control panel to show a mini drinks fridge. This was to keep drinks cool, particularly for long journeys.

He turned next, to the dome. This was a multi-purpose device, he explained. It could be rolled away leaving just a wind shield all the way round in the summer or parts of it could be rolled away when pods were linked. The dome could be darkened completely or just a bit to minimise the glare of the sun or when using the dome or wind shields as a monitor screen.

You could watch TV, videos, play computer games or read books or magazines, all from the extensive onboard library. There was also full internet capability built in for those that wanted to use the travelling time to do some work or just have some fun.

He finished the presentation by gracefully taking off in his pod and flying slowly off into the distance whilst he waved to his family below. The final scene showed him passing other single, double and multiple pods all travelling to unknown destinations.

33 STARTING WORK

Daisy & Phoebe were all smiles when the presentation finished.

'Wow, Molly, I LOVE it!'

'Me too! It seems so simple an idea. Much better than travelling for ages in a car'

'Or going 'cattle class' on a plane and having your space invaded by the selfish person in front throwing their chair back into your lap.'

'Yes, and waiting hours at the airport beforehand. It wouldn't have been possible without your pCell though Phoebe. I don't think you fully realise how it's opened everything up to radical new design'

'I suppose, I was concentrating so much on the fuel side of things and how easily things could be adapted, but I think you're right Mol, I didn't consider that so many new designs would now be possible.'

'What about the car and aircraft manufacturers though. Will you have as much trouble from them as Phoebe has had from the oil companies?'

'Well, not me personally, Daisy. Lady Catherine has taken the brunt of the criticism on my behalf of course, but she says the pCells have changed things for the better for so many people around the world that the small amount of grief she had at first from the oil companies was well worth it.'

'Don't worry, guys. The Travel Pods are different. These will be a commercial venture and not free as they aren't EXACTLY essential. Ms Drake and I have discussed this side of things and we intend to offer the design to various car and aircraft manufacturers to make them under licence for us. Hopefully this will keep them happy. Other manufacturers may adapt the design and bring out styles of their own but we already own the copyright so we would always receive recognition and payment if they do.

Talking of the design….'she thought instructions. 'There you are. I've sent the blueprints over to you. Tell me what you think and if you can see anything that could be done better'

The two girls were quiet while they studied the blue prints, concentration showing across their brows. After a while, Phoebe spoke first.

'Well I can't see anything I would change so far but I suppose you have been working with Ms Drake on the design for a while so I expect you've ironed out most of the problems'

'Yes, we've made several revisions so far but sometimes a fresh eye may pick something up'

'I think it's wonderful and so are you' Daisy had tears in her eyes.

'Now stop that now! Soppy Mare! It's one thing, working on paper but quite another to make it work in reality so we've got a lot of work ahead of us. Once we have a shell made, I've allocated us each a part of the project that we can be responsible for. We're going to make one single pod first. The accessory pods will all be based on this anyway.

Phoebe, I want you to be in charge of the anti-grav system, lighting, heating, mechanics, magnetic strips, please. Daisy, I want you to be responsible for the chair. Don't look like that, it's much more complicated than it looks. Also the safety features, anti-collision, the inflated net etc. I'll take care of the dome and the computer systems and link everything together.' The girls all nodded agreement.

'Right, lets get over to the workshop, our home for as long as it takes, and we'll get started on the mould for the shell'

34 WORK CONTINUES

Phoebe loved having another project to work on, even if she was not in charge this time. It felt good to let someone else take overall responsibility and she did have a bit of a soft spot for Molly. She was so much brighter than any of the other girls but had such a big generous heart!

Phoebe hoped that Freya would still join them as she really liked her too, but she was acting a bit strange just lately and Phoebe felt there was something more than just jealousy over her friendship with Molly. But every time she tried to read her, she put the barriers up to stop her, so Phoebe decided to give her some privacy.

Phoebe had been grateful to Freya when she first arrived. She had found it extremely difficult to let go of her protection of her Ants and Freya, who felt no such inhibitions, helped her immensely.

Phoebe was an only child and had been living with her mother and step father when she first came to the school. Her father had died just after she was born and her mother had remarried only a few years before her Ants arrived.

She had felt jealous of her step father at first, as she had not had to share her mother with anyone else up until then. She had thought they would always be that close but suddenly her mother was paying much more attention to this man, than to her.

It was only when she got her Ants that she began to understand her mother and how difficult it must have been for her as a single parent for all of these years, with little adult company. Although she still thought her mother could have handled things a bit better and not completely stopped some of the things they used to do together.

Her step father was quite good to her as it turned out. He was a tutor at the local college and had never been married before. He seemed to genuinely care about Phoebe and it was clear he was very much in love with her mum. Before long they were expecting an addition to the family and Phoebe was delighted when her beautiful little brother was placed in her arms for the first time.

When her Ants arrived, like all of the other girls that this scary phenomenon had happened to, she kept it to herself. Something in their super intelligence made them cope better than most would have.

She knew the first thing she had to do was to learn to control her hearing before she went mad. Next priority was her vision. At first she kept tripping over everything as her vision flipped from normal to microscopic to long distance, all in the space of a few minutes. She just managed to learn to control them in time to stop her mum from taking her to the hospital for tests.

Her parents had been more than a little stunned when Beth Drake contacted them about sending Phoebe to a special boarding school. Phoebe had been exceptionally good about hiding her Ants so they had no idea about them. Phoebe was puzzled too about how Ms Drake had found her. Ms Drake told her that she was now developing almost a sixth sense about girls with newly acquired Ants and Phoebe grew to be happy that she had.

****

The girls squealed with excitement when they turned the first pod out of it's mould. It looked perfect to them. The new combination of hard wearing materials they had used, seemed to have worked beautifully on the larger mould.

They had used their microscopic vision to look at the molecules of different materials to see what was likely to be a good mix. They then tried out the most promising in small moulds until Molly was finally happy that this was the one. The other girls learnt very quickly that Molly was a perfectionist where her project was concerned.

She didn't give them long to admire their handiwork before she went onto her next part which was the dome and the girls knew they were expected to get to work on their next allocated part of the project.

Over the next few weeks, work was intense, but the girls where perfectly happy with the way the project was going. Then one day, just as they were finishing off for the day, Freya walked into the workshop. None of them had seen much of her just lately. She was blocking them out but they didn't need their Ants to know she was nervous and something was wrong.

'Hi Freya! Whatever's the matter?'

'Nothing…..nothing at all, why?'

'Well you look awful'

'Thanks, I feel much better now. I'm fine. I've just had a few worries just lately, that's all, but everything's alright now.' She looked about to continue so the girls waited for her to speak again. 'I've had to delay my own project for a while so I was wondering if you still needed my help on yours Molly?'

'Erm….. yeah, of course, I think we could squeeze you in. Perhaps you could help Daisy with the safety features or Phoebe with the anti-grav or mag strips? Your choice.'

'Yes, thank you, Molly. I'll see you all tomorrow.' She turned to go.

'We're all eating together this evening to go over progress and update our To Do lists if you'd like to join us?'

Freya inexplicably looked frightened and answered far too quickly.

'I can't, sorry, I have plans already. I'll see you tomorrow' and she rushed out.

'Perhaps she's worrying about her first placement or can't decide on a career path. It's coming up to that time for her, isn't it? She's a bit older than the rest of us'

'I think there's more to it than that, Daisy. I've been close friends with her since I got here and she's even been keeping me at arm's length just lately. I've offered to be there for her and help her with any decisions she has to make but she got extremely agitated when I suggested she had a word with Ms Drake if something was bothering her'

'I think we ought to see how she goes tomorrow. I'm not being heartless, but I don't want her messing my project up. We've worked far too hard for that, but I am worried about her. I know she's blocking us but it's putting such a strain on her. She's trying to keep it up for much too long.'

'Yes, the rest of us aren't as good at it as you are Molls. You keep it up permanently with no effort at all. There would be no finding out your secrets!' They all smirked.

'Good job I don't have any then! I let you in when I want to, anyway. But seriously, rules or no rules, I'm getting such a bad vibe about her, if she's no better by the end of tomorrow, I'm breaking down her walls and I'll help her whether she wants me to or not.'

'Can you even do that?'

'Oh yes, if I have to!'

The girls didn't know whether to be proud of Molly or scared of her but were in fact a little bit of both.

35 FREYA

Freya had known all the comforts of life. Her family were very wealthy and had made their first money generations ago when an enterprising inventor, having failed to patent his vacuum cleaning device in time, had successfully gone into canning food.

Her house was very grand and she was extremely spoilt by her grandfather, (who she spent most of her early childhood with), despite the constant protests from her parents that he would turn her into a brat. This didn't happen, however, as Freya was always very level headed and really did appreciate that not everyone had what she had.

She felt like an only child as her brother, Danté, was fifteen years older than she, so they had nothing in common and barely saw each other. He worked in the family food business now with his parents, but he hated it. He was constantly looking for a way out and came up with scheme, after dodgy scheme, to make enough money to be independently wealthy in his own right.

Freya had often heard him arguing with their parents about money. Danté thought he shouldn't have to work and should have been given a generous allowance so he could travel the world and act like a spoilt playboy. Their parents would not allow him to waste his life this way and wanted him to be a productive, happy person who contributed to society. They offered to back him in any venture, and the family firm WAS just a stop gap, but he had never found anything worthwhile that he wanted to do with his life. He always just wanted to get rich quick.

Freya knew Danté had no idea when her Ants arrived and he was even oblivious when, some time later, she went away to school. She hadn't heard from him till months after she had arrived at Trescotham so she was very surprised by his call.

He had been looking for his parents to tell them about another crazy scheme he had thought up and had broken into his father's desk to check his diary. He had found a number for Freya in there but no diary. Freya told him his parents had gone away for a few days and he would have known that, if he had bothered to turn in for work or had managed to drag himself home.

She didn't hear from him for a while after that but next time he did contact her she would regret it with all her heart.

36 MOLLY INTERVENES

Freya turned up at the workshop the next day, just as she said she would, looking even more strung out than she had the day before. The girls started with their usual meeting about progress and tasks for the day (carried on from the previous night) and took the opportunity to update Freya on the nitty gritty of the project.

Molly sent the demo video and blueprints to her Think Dot and left her to study them while she and the girls went to their separate work stations to get on.

Daisy was still tinkering with the chair but had already started on the mag strips, so she asked her to show Freya where she was up to. Molly was keeping a close eye on Freya. She was still blocking them from reading her but Molly had already had a quick scan of her body to make sure she was not really ill. Everything was ok apart from the physical signs of illness that came along with mental stress, so no surprise there.

Molly had the dome all sorted and ready to tie in with the rest and was now working on the computer controls. She had been practising getting in and out of electronic systems using her unique ability with the help of Ms Franklyn. She had no problems now and had mastered yet another Ant. So now she could build the circuitry required, upload the software programme she had written especially for the project and test everything out and use her special skill whenever necessary to speed things up.

Freya seemed to be doing ok working with Daisy, and Phoebe also silently indicated to Molly that she thought so too. Freya seemed to relax a little but still didn't let her guard down.

By the end of the day, they all felt like further progress had been made and Molly said she thought they were close to being able to put everything together for the first time. The girls were very excited and they arranged to meet later for their usual evening meal and debrief and this time Freya agreed to come along.

They were on their way out of the door, when Molly stopped and froze almost in mid step. Phoebe and Daisy also sensed something and turned around to see what was going on. Molly had a look of deep concentration on her face and Freya had just turned to face her. It looked like a scene from an artist's painting, both girls just staring intensely at each other. No malice, just deep, deep concentration.

Then suddenly Freya screamed and collapsed in a heap on the floor, sobbing her heart out. All the girls rushed over to comfort her.

'Freya, whatever's the matter?', Freya couldn't speak.

'Phoebe, she's ok now. She dropped her guard a little and I managed to break through and find out what's going on with her. Let's take her back to her room. I'm sure she'd rather tell you everything herself'

In Freya's room, all the girls could do was stroke her hair and hold her hand until the racking sobs finally turned to intermittent sniffs. She had held things in so tightly for so long that once she let go, she thought she would die from crying. Daisy and Phoebe also felt her pain but only Molly knew the full story.

37 CONFESSIONS

Freya sat on the sofa in her room while the girls fussed over her and got her a drink.

'Whatever it is Freya, I'll always be your friend. You can tell me anything. It won't affect that'

'Thanks Pheebs but I think you'll change your mind when you find out what I've done'

'It can't be that bad. Start talking girly, spill the beans!' Daisy tried to lighten the atmosphere a bit. The girls sat around the room and waited for her to start.

'You all know I have a much older brother.'

'Yes, Danté isn't it?'

'Yes, that's right. Well, he's not like me and the rest of my family. He's always looking for cons or scams to pull to make him rich enough so he could move abroad and live a life of luxury. My parents have tried to instil the work ethic in him, even though we are quite wealthy, but I suppose he really is a, not very nice, black sheep of the family.' She paused to sip her drink again.

'There are a lot of families that have one of those.' Daisy thought of her big sister.

'We're not close, partly to do with the age gap I suppose and I'm certain he knew nothing about my Ants or the true nature of Trescotham, even when he broke into my father's desk and found my personal number. I think he just thought I had been sent away to boarding school. But from what I can gather, he overheard something at home and then planted listening devices around the house so he could find out more.

When we were launching the pCell, my parents discussed, in private, how proud they were of me for my part in its development and of course he heard' The girls were beginning to get the picture.

'He contacted me again and said he knew all about my super brain and I was his ticket to a new life.' Her voice faltered as she held back more sobs. 'He threatened to go to the papers and expose the school unless I let him know the details of any new projects that he could steal and sell to the highest bidder.

I didn't know what to do. I don't think he understands the true nature of all our abilities but I was mortified at the prospect of us being exposed to the rest of the world. I love my life here with all of you and I'm so proud of all the things we've accomplished. Things here MATTER if you know what I mean' Of course they did.

'So you told him about my Travel Pod'

'I've been feeding him little bits of worthless information for a while now but he was getting impatient and more threatening so I had to tell him about your project and this morning I sent him your blueprint. I'm so sorry Molly. I couldn't think of a way to stop him. All these Ants and I can't deal with my own obnoxious brother'

'Freya, please, I understand. It has been a terrible time for you. I hope you know I *had* to break through your barriers to help. I sensed the immense strain you were under and I knew it got worse when you came near us three and the project. So to be on the safe side I sent you a fake blueprint that couldn't possibly work. I had an inkling it was affecting your Ants so I thought you might not spot it with you being so pre occupied.'

'Molly, what a relief' her face showed it was short lived. 'But what about Danté? He'll expose us all!'

'Don't worry Freya! It'll be ages before he, or anyone he tries to sell them to, realises the plans won't work. We'll have plenty of time to sort him out before then'

'Sort him out? What do you mean by that?'

'Just that it's about time we put our training and our Ant's to good use in the real world and I think I have an idea how we can do just that!'

38 DANTÉ

Danté was thrilled his little sister had come through for him at last. He would sell these blueprints, arranging a cut of future profits at the same time of course, and he would never have to work again! Sun, sand, sea, surf and lots of girlfriends for him from now on.

Without Mummy and Daddy holding the purse strings, he would get the car HE wanted. About time too at nearly thirty years old! Maybe he'd even get two cars……Oh and a boat. Yes!! He'd always wanted a boat. He didn't have to wait for that. He had seen a beauty he liked and he could afford to hire it for a while till he got some money through. Then he'd buy it. It would certainly impress the ladies and help to establish his new playboy lifestyle.

His thoughts went back to his little sister. He hadn't finished with her yet. Why should he? She was scared stiff he would go to the papers about her and that freak school of hers. He'd sell the blueprints and then go back to her for more little gems. Why not? You could never have TOO much money.

Mmmmm, where to sell the blueprints. This wasn't going to be as easy as he'd thought. He'd already made a couple of tentative enquiries with car manufacturers, before he had the goods to back him up, but he got the impression they thought he was a crazy person......or on drugs. It might be a bit easier now he could show them the blueprints. He'd have to make some copies first though, and quickly. He only had them on his mobile at the minute and he would be stuffed if anything happened to that.

First things first. He'd go hire that boat. He needed somewhere of his own to lay low for a while anyway. He didn't want even more hassle from his parents about not turning in to the stupid office, so that would be ideal.

He threw some things into a holdall, grabbed his laptop and passport and jumped in his car. He stopped off to buy a couple of memory sticks and headed for the marina.

39 MORE DANTÉ

He sat on the deck, drinking beer from the bottle, wondering if the sun was going to come out at all today. He was pouring over maps looking for his first destination where the sun would definitely be shining. He couldn't wait to get his shirt off and get some red hot sun on his bones again.

He knew he was an extremely good looking man and loved the attention he got, especially with his toned muscles on display. After all, he worked hard at the gym to keep them in peak condition.

He was very tall and had almost black hair like his sister Freya, but where her eyes were very pale blue, his were very dark brown. He knew how to use his good looks to get what he wanted. Something his sister hadn't learned to do yet. He wouldn't have called himself vain, but others definitely did.

He'd almost decided on his first port of call when his phone rang. An unknown number.

'Y'ello. Danté Jerome's poodle parlour' his usual first words. He listened.

'Oh, right. Yep.....yep that's right, I have them here.............Yes, I'd love to meet up. Look I live on a boat moored up at the marina at present. How about you come down here this afternoon, say two o'clock and we could talk and perhaps have a little run out along the coast?...............Excellent. Bring lots of cash, ha ha!! My boat's moored at D56. I'll look out for you. Oh, what do you look like?................Mmmm, ok, see you later. Bye!'

Well his day was certainly looking up. A redhead was coming to see him this afternoon about the blueprints. He'd always had a thing about redheads. Hopefully it wouldn't be long before he had all that lovely money to spend.

40 DEALING WITH DANTÉ

The young woman walking down the quayside towards him, was indeed a stunner, as he had hoped. Her gorgeous long red hair was tied loosely at the nape of her neck and he could see her shapely figure even though she was attempting to hide it with her business attire. He was pleased to see she was carrying quite a large briefcase and hoped, but doubted, that it was filled with cash.

'Hello, Mr Jerome? I'm Beth Drake'

'Please, call me Danté. This is my humble home for the time being. Watch your step as you come aboard' He held out his hand to help steady her as she stepped onto the deck.

'Thank you, Mr J…Danté'

'May I get you something to drink?' his manners were impeccable at least.

'Just a glass of water will be fine, thank you' He raised his eyebrows in derision once he had turned away from her.

'Ok......Beth' he started, hesitating to see if she objected to him using her first name. 'I didn't ask you which company you are from. I have so many companies interested in the blueprints already, it's difficult to keep track. So expect to pay a premium price for them, if you're interested, or someone else will outbid you'

'I'm not from a company as such. I am the principle of Trescotham Hall, your sister's school' his face was a picture!

'Err.....Err....you tricked me. What're you gonna do? You'd better not call the police. I'll tell them and everyone else about your school and all the weirdoes that go there. I'm sure you don't want THAT getting out. They'll experiment on them and all sorts....' He ran out of steam.

'I don't think that is necessary, Mr.....Danté. I have thirty thousand pounds in my briefcase and I have been authorised to buy the blueprints back from you, along with your silence, and THIS TIME ONLY, we won't contact the police ourselves.'

'THIRTY THOUSAND POUNDS!!?? That's pathetic!! I could make MILLIONS, perhaps even BILLIONS.........'

'I don't think so. The plans you have are worthless. There is a deliberate flaw in them that can't be worked around.'

'What!! Impossible…….I don't believe it. Why offer to buy them back if they don't work? You're just saying that.'

'Do you want to take that risk?'

'For millions of pounds? I certainly think so. But you wouldn't take the risk of going to the police and exposing that precious school of yours. I think I'll take my chances'

'Good luck to you then, Mr Jerome'

Beth was about to get up and leave when the boat's engine suddenly fired up. Danté jumped up and went over to the controls.

'What do you think you're doing Mr Jerome?'

'Danté! And I'm not doing anything!' he sounded frantic.

The boat's engine noise increased slightly as the boat started to move away from the jetty. Danté was in full panic mode and was pressing buttons and flicking switches on the boats control panel, but to no avail.

'I can't stop it. What's happening'

'If this is some sort of trick Mr Jerome........'

'It's not me, I tell you!!' he screamed at her.

'There's a speed limit in this crowded area isn't there? You're going far too fast' By now they were heading at quite a rate, towards the exit of the marina towards the open sea. Several people along the quayside had stopped what they were doing and were now watching them with disapproval.

Suddenly a small rowing boat was right in their path. The three occupants seemed to be oblivious of the impending danger almost upon them. Danté screamed a warning at them, in vain. The wind carried his words in the opposite direction. All he could do was brace himself and watch as his boat cut the other one clean in half, tumbling its occupants into the water, to be hit full on by his hull.

Beth looked terrified. 'What have you done? You're a maniac! You've killed those people! Stop this boat now!' He tried the controls again and this time they responded.

They both peered over the side to see if they could see any survivors, but there wasn't even any wreckage visible. Danté ran frantically from one side of the boat to the other, hoping against hope that he would see three heads above the water asking to be pulled aboard……but there was nothing. Tick, tick, tick, tick…….still nothing.

'Oh my god, I can't believe this is happening. It wasn't me, I'm telling you. The boat just took off on its own. You'll be my witness, won't you? I was sitting with you when the engine started up'

'I'm afraid I don't know much about boats. Perhaps you didn't turn it off properly. You certainly looked like you were driving the boat once you were at the controls and it would have certainly looked that way to the people on the quayside. And why hadn't you put the mooring ropes over those capstans'

'I did. I remember doing it after I had a quick run out earlier. Oh I see…..OK, I see what you're up to. I won't tell anyone about the school. Just please back me up.'

'Thank you, but no matter what I say, there are still plenty of other witnesses'

He suddenly turned his head and pricked up his ears. He could hear the faint sound of police sirens.

'Someone's called the police. I'm not getting the blame for this. I hope you can swim.' With that he pushed Beth Drake into the water, threw the life belt after her and sped off for the open water.

41 AFTERMATH

'Are you girls ok?'

'Yep, that was great fun'

'But not without risk!'

'We know, but a risk worth taking. I don't think we'll be seeing your brother round here again, Freya. Not as long as he thinks he's a fugitive and would be arrested. Not to mention stealing a boat he's only supposed to have hired'

'Yes, Molls, thank goodness, but knowing him, that thirty thousand pounds won't last him very long'

'No, but that's up to him. He's old enough to fend for himself and make his own living…..or not, as the case may be.' They all chuckled and suspected they knew which it would be.

Beth Drake had just come back from thanking one of her ex pupils, Chief Inspector Lucy Ford for her part in the sting. She had arranged for two squad cars with sirens blazing, to arrive at just the right time. She had then calmed the onlookers by telling them they had just watched a scene being shot for a new tv movie, and would they now move along please. The Alumni of Trescotham would do anything asked of them to protect their beloved school.

'That was a great bit of acting, Ms Drake. You really did sound scared'

'I always loved drama at school but it wasn't all an act. I was very concerned about you three in the row boat, in case any of you wouldn't manage to get out of the way in time and our boat had hit you. And there was Molly to worry about, underneath our boat, working the controls. So, I just imagined the worse had happened to help with my acting. Did you manage to wipe his phone and delete any copies, Molly?'

'Yes, I only wiped the blueprint and Freya's number from his phone and wiped the one memory stick he'd managed to copy it to. Well at least we know now that THAT particular Ant also works under water. I did wonder'

'Yes, maybe we should have thought to test it beforehand but there was no time. We would have had to try something else, pretty quickly if it hadn't worked. We're still monitoring his phone though and we'll continue to do so wherever he ends up, just in case he decides it's safe to return home.'

'I have to admit, I had butterflies in my tummy from when I saw Molly slip the mooring ropes off. I knew we had to be ready from then and listen for Molly's signal to jump, but it's the first time I've ever done anything quite like this and it could have all gone so wrong. I know our underwater rescue training helped but somehow this was different. It was us that were in REAL danger'

'None of us have done this before either, Daisy. Not for real. Has it put you off? Were you too scared to ever do anything like this again?'

'I didn't say that Pheebs! Bring it on!!!!!'

They finished getting changed into their dry clothes and made their way back to the car and the flasks of hot tea they had thankfully thought to bring with them. They couldn't help but feel a twinge of sorrow for Danté, but they felt this was the best way to protect the school and Freya, from him. So the sorrow soon turned to contentment as they sat in silence, each with their own thoughts, as, with every mile, the car took them closer to *home*.

42 FINISHED PROJECT

All four girls worked even harder over the next few weeks. They knew the end was in sight.......or the beginning as they all thought of it. The prototype was really taking shape and they were almost ready to give it a full test run.

Lady Catherine had already lined up several manufacturers who were interested in being licensed to produce the vehicles and they were due to come to a demonstration at her estate in two weeks time. It was vital the pod be ready and fully tested by then. The team would have been very excited but they were far too busy to think that far ahead.

If everything went to plan, Molly and the team were to train several of the older girls, who were ready to find placements, so that they could oversee the new technology once production started. Molly had been aware all the way through that Norms would eventually have to build her pods so she had to be very careful that the process wasn't possible purely by using Ants.

Finally, they were ready to put the prototype Travel Pod through its paces. Molly had gone over every micrometer to make sure everything was as it should be before she took it for its first test drive.

They all giggled at each other in excitement as they stood on the grass.

'I suppose I ought to say a few words before we start'

'What, final words before you die!'

'Cheeky! No, I just want to say thank you to all of you, my BFFs. I KNOW the last F is so true. We're going to be part of each others lives FOREVER.' They had a group hug as tears welled up in their incredible eyes.

'Right, less of the mush, lets get testing!'

Molly took a deep breath and gave the command 'Open Door'. She could have placed her palm next to the door to have the same effect, which they had already tested, but this was her preferred method of entry.

The door slid away as the seat turned towards her and lowered itself to the perfect pre-set height for Molly. She sat down and the seat turned her towards the control panel as the door slid shut. She had to resist the temptation to use her Ants as the pod was designed for Norms to use.

She had pre programmed the sat nav to take her on a round trip of the grounds only. She couldn't risk flying above the holographic projection system in case she was seen, so it was going to be a very low level flight. She gave the command 'Follow Route' and held her breath as the pod slowly began to rise and the legs turned horizontally and tucked themselves away out of sight. She was airborne! It was a beautifully smooth ride and she felt almost majestic.

The girls on the ground were monitoring every aspect of the pod on their Think Dots and kept in constant contact with Molly. Everything looked within expected tolerances so far. They waved to her as she began to slowly move away. Molly had to stop herself from marvelling at the view while she was up there. This was work. There would be plenty of time for a pleasure trip later on.

She wanted to test the anti-collision sensors so she had placed several obstructions along the route. The pod handled them with no trouble, even the one she had spring up suddenly out of a tree. The sudden swerve was smoothed out and as a passenger, she still felt very comfortable.

She tested the entertainment system out again using the control panel as well as voice control and darkened and lightened the dome. She then drew the dome back leaving just the wind shields in place. This time she allowed herself a few minutes to enjoy the ride with the wind dancing in her hair before she continued testing.

She was highly delighted with the first test run so far. She had programmed a short stop to test the landing system and once airborne again she just had the inflated net to try out. Molly was such a stickler for detail and the very few teething troubles they had had along the way, she had sorted them out immediately, so she was not expecting the net to fail. However, her intelligence stopped her from being too over confident as there was always a small chance something unpredictable could go wrong.

She was almost back to the girls when she gave them the instruction to turn the anti-grav system off. She knew they were all nervous, particularly Daisy, whose responsibility it had been.

For a split second, nothing happened and she could feel the pressure of gravity pulling her back towards the ground even before the pod started to move downwards.

Then woosh!! The net enclosed the whole pod and inflated itself in one quick movement. Molly just felt a soft bump as they landed a short distance from where the girls were now doing a crazy victory dance.

Molly gave the command to repack the net and return the pod back to normal land mode and she then manually drove it back to the workshop for the debrief.

'Wow, that was fantastic Molls. How did the emergency landing feel?'

'Fine, just a soft sort of bump. You did a great job Daisy. It absorbed all the impact so it didn't carry on bouncing. And the chair was super comfy too!! We'll go over the readings but so far there's just one thing I want to tweak'

'What's that?'

'I want that net to deploy much faster. It nearly made my heart stop!'

Not for the first time, they collapsed into fits of laughter.

43 ANOTHER SURPRISE

They spent the time until the trial with testing, testing and more testing until they were happy everything was perfect. Of course they were not allowed to be seen at the demonstration. Lady Catherine had her own staff to take responsibility for the design. The girls always knew this was the only way and were ok with it. Their ages would certainly have raised suspicions. The girls watched and listened though from a safe distance.

The manufacturers were extremely impressed and excited about the pods and Lady Catherine, with her keen business sense and incredible people skills, had no trouble getting them to agree to go into production as soon as possible.

She held a large party at her home to celebrate. All the girls and staff at the school had been invited. It was spectacular. Molly had never seen such a do in her life and she and her team were treated like royal guests at a celebration ball.

Molly was sure that even without her total recall, she would have remembered every minute of that beautiful evening. She would also have remembered that it was the next day she had a conversation that would have incredible implications for them all.

She was having a lazy day. She thought she deserved it after all the hard work they had all done. She was thinking she might go home for a week or two. That would please Mum. She had only had chance for quick chats on the Think Dot for weeks. They had been very excited and proud that her pod was finally finished and would soon be going into production. They intended to be one of the first families to own some as they were expected to be so very cheap.

Then her ringtone sounded in her ear and on her command, her brother's face appeared in front of her eyes.

'Hi H! What's up? You must have read my mind. I was just about to call you guys' She knew her little brother wasn't himself.

'Molls, I need to talk to you but don't tell Mam and Dad....or Lucas'

'Okaaay. Sounds mysterious. You know I have to tell them if you've done anything illegal!'

'Very funny! Just shut up and listen to me for once' Molly waited and couldn't quite believe what her senses were telling her, even over this distance. Harry hesitated, not sure how to put it into words. Then he decided to just come out with it.

'Molly.........I've developed Ants!'

ABOUT THE AUTHOR

Anne Braid lives with her husband Garry in North East Lincolnshire. They have 3 grown-up daughters 2 granddaughters and 3 grandsons (so far!). Anne loves reading all types of books, particularly crime/thrillers, both on paper and on her Kindle. She loves technology but wishes it was far more advanced than it is now.